A MURDER IN MAYFAIR
A VICTORIAN HISTORICAL MYSTERY

ROSALYND & STEELE MYSTERIES
BOOK ONE

MAGDA ALEXANDER

HEARTS AFIRE PUBLISHING

PROLOGUE
LONDON

MARCH 1889

The tavern in Spitalfields was a low den, more a place of desperate refuge than any reputable establishment. London's evening gloom had settled heavily over the crooked streets, pressing the stale reek of industrial smoke and damp stone into every crevice. Inside, the small common room glowed a sickly yellow from oil lamps and tallow candles. It wasn't a place frequented by the respectable; even the most indifferent watchmen knew better than to linger here. Yet, at one corner table, a curious meeting was taking place.

Seated at that grimy table were two men who, at a casual glance, could not have appeared more different. The first, clearly a gentleman, was dressed in a well-tailored suit of fine cloth, a waistcoat of deep burgundy beneath a black frock coat, and trousers pressed with meticulous care, seemed misplaced in this den of broken souls. A gleaming silver pocket watch hung on a chain, and on his lapel was a pin that might have been a family crest. He had positioned himself so as to touch the table as little as possible, grimacing discreetly each time a drop of stale ale or some unnameable sticky residue threatened to soil his cuffs. His face was sharp, hawkish. A low-slung cap shadowed keen grey eyes that spoke of an intellect sharpened by privilege and a first-rate education. The slight curl of his lip at the corners betrayed a man accustomed to finer establishments.

Opposite him was a fellow who seemed born from the muck and mire of Spitalfields itself. Tall, broad, thick-necked, built like a butcher. A scar marred the right side of his face. He wore a grimy shirt whose original color was long lost to sweat and soot. His jacket—torn at the elbows and stained with who knew what—barely kept out the chill of the evening. His trousers, similarly tattered, bore silent witness to a life lived close to the gutter. His hair was ragged and dull, his fingernails chipped and blackened with dirt. He smelled of rancid meat and stagnant rainwater. His eyes, though, were sharp in their own way—a feline brightness that suggested cunning and hunger.

Their tankards of ale stood between them as a meager truce. The upper-class toff had avoided drinking the swill. The other man, known as O'Donnell to the few who cared to remember it, had downed half his tankard in a few gulps. The ale, cheap and bitter, was a comfort to him in a world without many comforts.

The toff leaned forward slightly, lowering his voice so that it would not carry beyond their table. "I trust that we have reached a suitable understanding?"

O'Donnell wiped a drip of ale from his scruffy beard. The amber droplet caught on the candlelight before disappearing into the coarse hairs. "Aye," he said in a voice that rasped like a file on iron. "We understand each other well enough. Ye want a certain gentleman put in the ground. I'm willing to do that, fer a price."

The toff inclined his head, as if acknowledging a minor point in a contract.

"The target is neither stout nor slim, about fifty years of age. He is well-dressed—always in a dark coat—and favors a red scarf. This scarf should help you identify him at once. He's no fool and keeps careful habits, but I know where he will be. He frequents the home of Evangeline Pratt, his mistress, on Tuesday and Thursday evenings. She lives in a small house off Princelet Street, well within your reach. On those nights, he will be there shortly after nightfall, savoring what comfort he can find there that he can't find at home."

O'Donnell chuckled darkly. "I'm not after a full life's story, guv. Just enough to know the right man. Ye can leave the details of how to me."

The upper-class man nodded again, pulling his gloved hands away from the sticky table. He seemed eager to conclude this business. "Of course. I merely wish no mistakes. There's a legacy hanging in the balance. If this goes well, there will be another task for you."

"As long as it isn't a lass or a babe, I'm your man."

"Not even for a hundred pounds?" the toff smirked.

O'Donnell neither agreed nor disagreed, but the avarice in his eyes gleamed clearly. With enough coin, he could be bought.

Silence settled over them for a moment. The tavern's other patrons—drunks, petty thieves, and broken laborers—were lost in their own grim worlds. A lamplight flickered, casting shadows that danced across the warped floorboards. Outside, a distant cry sounded, perhaps a cat, perhaps something more human. This was London's underbelly, and these men were playing a deadly game in its shadows.

"Well then," said O'Donnell, leaning forward. "There's the matter of payment."

Reaching into his coat with deliberate care, the toff drew forth a small pouch.

O'Donnell watched with a predator's interest, eyes narrowing. "As agreed upon," said the toff, "here are twenty pounds in coin. The remainder will be paid upon the successful completion of your task."

With a gloved hand, he slid the pouch across the table. O'Donnell did not snatch it greedily, not yet. He was a professional, in his own grim way, and such eagerness could be misconstrued. Instead, he drew the pouch toward himself with two fingertips, opening it just enough to glimpse the glint of metal inside. Satisfied, he closed it again and slipped it into the pocket of his trousers.

"That'll do for now," the rough man said. He finished his ale in one long swallow, wiping his mouth on his sleeve. A thick silence settled again, broken only by the clink of tankards and the low hum of muttered conversations around them.

The toff cleared his throat. "You will find me at the address we discussed. After the deed is done, I will have the remainder of your fee."

O'Donnell's eyes narrowed, and he leaned in, lowering his voice to an almost inaudible growl. "I'll find ye all right. But mark me, ye'd best have that money ready. No excuses, no delays. If I show up and find ye've flown, or if ye try to be clever and wriggle out of this arrangement..." He paused, letting the implication hang in the sour air. "Let's just say I know where you live. And I know enough to ruin more than your fancy suit."

The toff's face tightened. This was the part of the transaction he disliked most: the acknowledgement that the gutter-snake he'd hired could just as easily turn on him. Yet, he needed O'Donnell's services, and in this matter, he had no other reliable means. He lifted his chin and tried to speak with calm authority. "Your warning is duly noted. Rest assured, I am a man of honor, and I will pay what I owe."

O'Donnell laughed silently, shoulders shaking. The notion of honor among these kinds of dealings was laughable, and they both knew it. "A man of honor," he echoed, mocking. "A man of your breeding wouldn't be here if he could soil his gloves in a more respectable manner, would he?"

The toff's jaw tightened. "I am here because I must be. The world is not always governed by polite rules. You know that better than most, I imagine."

O'Donnell smirked, revealing a few yellowed teeth. "So we have an understanding, then. I do this deed, and you pay me what's due. If not . . ." He let his voice trail off. The threat needed no repetition. The implication was enough—the toff's blood could just as easily join that of the target in the gutters of the East End.

The toff tried not to let the fear show in his face. Instead, he affected a mild indifference. "Indeed, we are in agreement. Now, I suggest we both be on our way. The night grows old, and I have other engagements. You have your... preparations to make."

O'Donnell rose from the table first. He stood a head taller than the toff and much heavier in build. He picked up his cap from a peg on the wall and settled it low over his brow. With a final look at the other man, he said, "Don't worry, guv. I'll get the job done. Lord High and Mighty will be feeding the fishes soon enough, or my name ain't Ratty O'Donnell."

With that, he sauntered toward the door. Moving fluidly through the cramped space, he navigated overturned stools and unconscious patrons as if he belonged here—because he did. The door creaked as he pushed it open, letting in a draft of cool night air that made the lamps flicker. A moment later, he was gone, swallowed by the darkness and the maze of alleys beyond.

The gentleman remained seated a moment longer. The coins were gone, twenty pounds already spent. The next time he and O'Donnell met, the job would be done—or at least, it had better be. He tried not to think about what would happen if O'Donnell failed, or if he tried to extract further payment through blackmail or violence. A shudder crawled up his spine. The idea that this filthy murderer knew where he lived—knew even the pattern of his doorstep—was unsettling in the extreme.

He came to his feet and made his way out. The pact was sealed. Twenty pounds had changed hands, and a man's fate was marked.

In 1889 London, deals were struck not only in counting houses and boardrooms, but also in grimy taverns with tankards of foul ale. He pushed open the door and stepped into the darkness. As the fog swallowed him, the city itself seemed to hold its breath, waiting for the inevitable violence that would soon follow.

CHAPTER ONE

ROSEHAVEN HOUSE

SUFFRAGE FOR WOMEN

"The right to vote!" Lady Whitworth exclaimed. "That's what we should demand from Parliament. Don't you agree, Lady Rosalynd?"

It wasn't the first time Lady Whitworth had urged me to adopt her point of view. But as the president of the Society for the Advancement of Women, I could not take sides before a vote was taken. So I chose the politic option. "An important issue most certainly, but there's another just as vital."

Miss Moore was not slow to take my hint. "What good would it do to demand the right to vote if we can't manage our own finances?"

"Well, obviously, once we obtain women's suffrage, we can advocate for the other matter," Lady Whitworth retorted, firm in her conviction.

After an hour of debating the subject of our petition to the House of Lords, we were no closer to a decision. While one faction had strongly argued we should demand women's suffrage, the other clamored for a woman's financial independence. You'd think, by now, I'd grown used to the loud disagreements. But this month's meeting had turned particularly fractious. So much so, we were at risk of not reaching a decision at all. And that I couldn't allow.

With more force than was necessary, I brought down the gavel on the round table that served as a podium. "We've been arguing both sides long enough, ladies. It's time to settle the issue once and for all."

"Hear, hear!" several of those present agreed.

Ignoring the throbbing ache between my brows, I said, "Lady Whitworth, if you would present your case."

"The right to vote is the most important. Once it's given to married women who've achieved the age of reason—"

"Reason? Ha!" the dowager Countess of Sheffield cried out. "Some women never manage that, no matter their age."

"Now, Hetty, we can't petition for our right to command our own destiny if we think other ladies are too stupid to vote," her sister, Lady Cosgrove, said.

The dowager stared down her nose at her sibling. "That's the argument the gentlemen will make, Fanny. That we have nothing but air between our ears. Why, just this past Thursday, I overheard a group of gentlemen discussing that very topic at Lady Berkeley's ball."

"What gentlemen?" Lady Whitworth demanded. Her fiery gaze threatened retribution to those who'd dared to espouse such a view.

"What does it matter?" The dowager responded. "They all share the same views. They think we're idiots."

I banged down the gavel again. "We're straying off topic, ladies." Again. I pointed to the younger woman who'd brought up the finances issue. "Miss Moore, please plead your case."

"Thank you, Lady Rosalynd." She came to her feet and turned to face those assembled. "We need to be able to direct our own funds. Having a man manage our money is a recipe for disaster. They have been known to mismanage our assets, and worse, abscond with them." No surprise why she was concerned. She'd inherited a fortune from her railroad tycoon father. "Why, I have to apply to my business manager if I wish to purchase so much as a hatpin." Having had her say, she returned to her seat.

"But why can't we petition for both the right to vote and the right to manage our own finances?" one of our newest members asked.

"Because men's minds are too simple to focus on more than one thing at a time, dear," the dowager declared.

Giggles and the occasional snort made their way around their room.

"We've dithered long enough," Lady Whitworth's voice boomed out. "I call for a vote."

Finally! No one wanted this matter settled more than me. But first, I needed to explain the guidelines under which a choice would be made. "Now, ladies, the vote will decide how we move forward with our petition. Option one is women's suffrage. Option two is the right to manage our own finances. You can only vote for one. Is that understood?"

Heads decorated with bird's nests, floral arrangements, and one rather odd fruit basket wavered in the air.

"How many wish to petition Parliament for a woman's right to vote?"

Out of twenty ladies present, fifteen raised their hands.

Even though it was a foregone conclusion which side

would carry the day, procedure required I ask, "How many want to plead for the right to manage her own finances?"

Four palms shot up.

With a great deal of satisfaction, I banged down the gavel one final time. "The right to vote petition carries the day."

A round of applause and huzzahs circled the room.

Miss Moore seemed so crestfallen, I had to say, "Don't lose heart, Miss Moore. Once the women's suffrage matter is successfully concluded, we'll petition for women's financial independence. In the meantime, would you like to draft what you would like to see in it?"

Miss Moore brightened up. "Thank you, Lady Rosalynd. I'll do that."

"But how will we petition Parliament?" Lady Barlow asked. Married less than a year, and by all accounts deeply in love, she'd been too occupied with her wifely duties to attend our last meeting. They seemingly had been successful as she appeared to be increasing.

The dowager patted her hand. "It's already been decided, dear. Lady Rosalynd will write the plea and see that it's delivered to the House of Lords."

"Anyone in particular?" Lady Barlow asked.

"It will be sent to the Legislation Committee, where it will be assigned to one of its members," I explained.

"Let us hope it's a peer with a liberal mindset," Lady Whitworth asserted. "A conservative would kill it stone dead."

"Indeed," I said.

After the meeting adjourned, I proceeded to the morning room to write the first draft of the petition. I wanted to note the points raised during our meeting while they were fresh on my mind. I entered the space to find one of our downstairs maids holding one of the miniatures on my desk.

"Begging your pardon, milady." Her face turned a bright shade of pink as she returned it to its place.

I offered her a smile to show I was not offended. "Maisie, is it not?"

"Yes, milady." She curtsied. "I didn't mean to pry. They're so beautiful, the little paintings."

"Glad you like them, Maisie. The miniatures of my family are very dear to me."

"I wish I had one of my mum. She was quite beautiful when she was younger."

If her mother resembled Maisie she indeed would have been quite stunning. Even in her maid's uniform and her dark hair tightly pinned into a bun, she couldn't hide her beauty. "Maybe it's not too late for a likeness."

The corners of her mouth turned down. "She's quite ill, milady, and not expected to live much longer. She would not want one taken of her now."

"I'm so sorry." I knew the pain she felt. My mother, along with my father, had been tragically taken from us six years ago.

A fearful expression rolled over her face. "I should go before Mrs. Bateman catches me jabbering."

"We wouldn't want that," I agreed with a laugh. Our housekeeper wasn't a martinet by any means, but she was strict about preserving a certain distance between the Rosehaven family and its staff. Familiarity was not allowed. "She'd likely frown at us both."

"Indeed, milady." One more curtsy, and she was gone.

During the next while, I worked diligently on the petition. So much so, I lost track of time.

I would have remained at my task for hours if not for my

youngest sister, Petunia. Without so much as a knock on the door, she burst into the room, a disgruntled expression on her gamine face. "It's teatime, Rosie. Aren't you coming?"

I glanced at the clock on the fireplace mantel. "Heavens! Is it four already?"

"Yes, it is. We can't start without you, and I'm *starving*." She flashed a grin that was lacking a tooth.

I came to my feet and swung her around. "You're always starving, poppet."

"I can't help it," Petunia said after I placed her safely on the ground. "I'm growing like a weed."

I propped my hands on my hips. "And who, pray tell, made that inappropriate remark?"

"Cosmos."

Our oldest brother. An expert botanist who tended to associate most things with his chosen vocation.

"That was very improper of him."

"I like it. He notices me."

"Of course, he does." She was such a lively child, no one could help but notice her. "Now let's get you fed before you *starve!*"

Giggling, she curled her hand around mine.

As we made our way to the drawing room, there was some skipping involved. At seven years of age, Petunia possessed an exuberant spirit that wasn't still for long. We arrived to find most of our other siblings, as well as our grandmother, the dowager Countess of Rosehaven, already there. Every Monday, she joined us for tea, ostensibly to spend time with her grandchildren. Chastising me for my sad lack of husband was an added treat.

"Good afternoon, Grandmother," I said, kissing her cheek. "I trust you're in good health."

"Other than a pair of creaking knees and the occasional heart flutter, I'm fit as a fiddle." With her impeccably arranged silver hair and her snapping black eyes, she made an imposing figure. And that was before she expressed one of her decided opinions.

"You'll outlive us all, ma'am," I said.

"Seeing how I'm seventy-six years of age, I doubt that very much." She was eighty-one, not that she'd ever admit it.

"My new gowns arrived," Chrissie whispered as I settled next to her on a sofa. Having reached the age of eighteen, my next younger sister was making her debut this season and couldn't be more excited.

"That's wonderful, Chrissie."

"What's that?" Grandmother asked in her booming voice. Along with creaking knees and heart flutters, she was hard of hearing.

"The modiste delivered my new evening dresses, Grandmother," Chrissie said in a louder voice.

"Good thing you're making your debut this year. If you'd waited much longer, you would have turned into a spinster." She narrowed her gaze at me. "Like your sister."

"Chrissie was suffering from a chest complaint last year, Grandmother, so I felt it best to wait."

"With her beauty and charm, Chrysanthemum would have snagged Lord Barlow. But because she wasn't there, the Whittier girl stole the march on her. What he saw in that insipid chit is beyond me."

"He fell in love."

The dowager stamped her cane on the floor. "He could have fallen in love with your sister just as well."

"Chrissie will not lack for suitors, Grandmother. Other

eligible gentlemen do exist." Offering my sister a soft smile, I patted her hand.

"You think so, Rosie?" Chrissie asked shyly.

"I know so." Who could not help but be attracted to her sweet disposition and winsome smile, never mind her strawberry gold tresses and aquamarine gaze. She was a beauty in every sense of the word.

Thankfully, Grandmother ceased her fire long enough for everyone to enjoy the wonderful repast. Scones, sandwiches, fairy cakes, and her favorite, oolong tea.

"How was your meeting, Rosie?" Chrissie asked while everyone was busy satisfying their hunger.

"We decided to send our petition for women's suffrage to the House of Lords. I've been writing the first draft."

"Which I'm sure will be splendid," Chrissie said.

"Thank you for saying that, dear."

Pursing her lips, Grandmother vigorously stirred a lump of sugar into her cup. "I don't know how you expect to marry, Rosalynd. Not only are you dangerously close to being firmly on the shelf, but you've gained a reputation as a reformer *and* a bluestocking. No gentleman of breeding will offer for you."

I sighed. We'd held the same discussion so many times I'd lost count. "I don't intend to marry, Grandmother, as you know."

She cast a gimlet eye on me. "And what pray tell do you mean to do with your life?"

"I will continue to attend to my sisters' studies and well-being, as well as Fox's. As you can see," I gazed around the room at my siblings, most of whom were busy scarfing down the food, "they lead very contented lives."

"Their upbringing is Cosmos's responsibility, not

yours." My older brother had inherited the earldom after our father's death. While he'd taken on the financial and estate management duties that came along with the title, the responsibility for our younger siblings' upbringing had fallen to me.

"He's busy with his botanical efforts, ma'am."

"Plants and flowers? What sort of vocation is that for a grown man? And an earl at that?"

"He's an expert on the subject, so much so, Scotland Yard regularly consults with him. Why, just last week, they approached him about a substance discovered during a postmortem. His expertise helped the police prove the victim had been poisoned by his wife."

"Postmortem? You mean a dead body?"

"Well, I certainly hope he was dead before they cut into him."

Grandmother's brows took a hike. "You have no sensibilities, my girl." Leaning heavily on her cane, she came to her feet. "I'm taking my leave. The Sowerby soiree is tonight, and I need my rest." She might be in her eighties, but she enjoyed a busy social schedule. "Don't forget we are to attend Lady Cholmondley-Smith's ball on Thursday."

"I won't." I stood as well. "Children, come say goodbye to your grandmother." They swarmed around her skirts, some no doubt leaving sticky fingermarks on her gown. But her gaze softened as she patted heads and kissed cheeks. As much of a martinet as she appeared to be, she had a soft spot for the children.

When she and I said our goodbyes at the house entrance, she turned a kind gaze on me. "You'll miss them, you know, once they're grown and leave the nest."

"I'll play aunt to their children."

Her gaze filled with pity. "It won't be enough, Rosalynd, not nearly enough. Beware lest you end up all alone, wondering where your life went wrong."

CHAPTER TWO

LADY CHOLMONDLEY-SMITH'S BALL

Going by the crush of bodies in Lady Cholmondley-Smith's ballroom, the second ball of the season was a smashing success. One could hardly walk through the throng without the fear of stepping on toes.

If I had my druthers, I would have gladly stayed home, reading a book, while enjoying a cup of strong tea. But as Chrissie's older sister, I had a duty to perform—shepherding her through the myriad of social events. Even this early in the season, she'd proven to be a popular debutante. So much so, her dance card had been filled within minutes of our arrival. It didn't surprise me in the least. She was beautiful, intelligent, and a wonderful conversationalist, mainly because she let the gentlemen do all the talking. As long as she listened, nodded, and occasionally exclaimed, "How wonderful," they were satisfied.

"Heavens, what a crush!" Lady Claire Edmunds exclaimed once we found each other. One of my closest friends, she and I had made our debut eight years ago. Highly sought after during that season, she'd received several offers of marriage. Her father had chosen a wealthy marquis in need of an heir. The fact he'd been in his fifties, drank copiously, and suffered from gout had not been taken into account. Two years ago, he'd keeled over during a vigorous bout of lovemaking, leaving Lady Claire with a country estate, a Mayfair mansion, and a generous widow's jointure.

"It is rather," I answered vigorously fanning myself. Due to the multitude of bodies, the air was downright steamy, something I abhorred. "Let us walk toward the terrace. There should be cooler air there by its doors."

"You do look a bit flushed." After linking arms, we made our way around the perimeter of the room. Along the way, we were greeted with nods and smiles, but didn't stop until we reached our destination.

The air indeed was noticeably cooler by the terrace, even though its doors remained closed. "Oh, that's better." I never could stand the heat.

"You'd think with this many people there'd be at least one interesting man in sight," Claire said, glancing around.

A grieving widow, she was not. And I couldn't blame her. After years of servitude to a randy peer, she was thoroughly enjoying her freedom.

Her gaze suddenly narrowed. "Oh, wait. One just arrived."

"Who?"

"The Duke of Steele. By the receiving line." She turned to me. "You've heard of him, of course."

"Actually, I've made his acquaintance. We were both at Needham Manor during the festivities surrounding Lady Eleanor's Christmas Ball." Lady Eleanor, my dearest friend, had not only invited me but demanded I attend, claiming I needed a respite from my familial duties.

"You didn't share *that* news with me," Claire said, somewhat surprised.

Knowing she would make a great deal of it, I'd decided to keep my own counsel. But, of course, I couldn't tell her that. Last thing I wanted was to hurt her feelings. "I've been so busy with Chrissie's debut, it slipped my mind."

She accepted my explanation with an amused smile. But clearly, her curiosity had been piqued. "So, how did you find him?"

"Aloof. Arrogant." And much too fascinating. But Lady Claire did not need to know that last part.

My friend glanced toward the receiving line once more. "Yes, he does have that reputation. He's also reportedly brilliant."

"So I've heard." Actually, I had not only heard but knew. Just prior to my arrival at Needham Manor, Lady Eleanor's diamond necklace had been stolen. The duke and I had both been asked to investigate. The successful conclusion of the matter, and our roles in it, had been kept from the holiday guests to keep the scandal from leaking out. But I'd discovered he was indeed highly intelligent. Unfortunately, he'd also turned out to be charming and fascinating. To tell the truth, he'd rather unsettled me. Once the festivities ended, I'd been glad to return home.

"He's rather striking, don't you think?"

Yes, he was. But I had no desire to share that opinion with Claire. She would make much more of it than I desired. So I simply asked another question. "You can see him from here?" We were standing on the opposite side of the room. With the press of bodies between us and the entrance, it would be difficult to note anyone's presence.

"You can't miss him as tall as he is, and then there's that white streak in his dark hair." She turned back to me. "Rumor has it he's in between mistresses at the moment."

That got my attention. "How do you know such a thing?"

"Afternoon teas. You'd know as well if you involved yourself in something other than children's nappies and women's suffrage."

"I've never been interested in gossip. And I'll have you know not one of my siblings is still in leading strings, much less nappies."

"But you do dedicate a huge amount of time to women's suffrage."

"Of course, I do. How else are we going to obtain the vote unless we keep pushing for it?" I let out a frustrated sigh. "We missed you at the meeting this week."

She raised and lowered both shoulders. "I was at the modiste. It was the only time she could fit me in." She squeezed my arm. "I promise to make the next one."

"Ummm," was my only response. She did support the cause, not as fervently as I did, but enough.

Her avid gaze returned to the receiving line. "The duke is quite in demand, you know. Every hostess worth her salt has sent him an invitation to her ball. It's quite a coup for Lady Cholmondley-Smith that he honored her with his presence."

"Why do they desire his attendance?" True, he was a duke, but so were others. What made him such a hoped-for guest?

She smirked. "Other than he's a duke who inherited the vast Steele fortune, you mean?"

Of course, she'd know all about that. But I couldn't let her get the better of me. "Yes. Other than that."

"He's a widower with no heir to the title. Other than his younger brothers, that is. Sooner or later, he must marry if he wants the Steele line to continue through him."

I'd discovered last Christmas he had no desire to marry again. But apparently, most of society, including Claire, were not aware of this. "So every lady in search of a husband has set her sights on him?"

"Exactly. As soon as our hostess let it be known he would be in attendance, every unattached female in town clamored for an invitation."

"That would explain the crush," I said, gazing around the room.

"It would be no hardship to be married to such a man. Not only would his wife be a duchess, but she'd be well entertained in bed."

My gaze snapped back to her. "I thought you despised marital relations."

"My husband was in his fifties, who had . . . difficulty performing, although it didn't stop him from trying. If rumors are anything to go by, Steele does not suffer from such a problem. Just the opposite, in fact."

"How do you know?"

She turned back to me. "Ladies talk, Rosalynd."

"What ladies?"

"The ones who've bedded him, of course."

"So he hops from bed to bed pleasuring ladies along the way? He must be quite busy."

"He has mistresses."

"More than one?" Steele had to have superb stamina.

She laughed. "Not at the same time. Honestly, Rosalynd, you have to socialize more. Then you'd learn a thing or two."

As busy as I was, the last thing I wanted was to engage in more social activities than I already did.

"In truth, I think he misses his wife," Claire continued. "She died in childbirth after only one year of marriage. Don't you recall? It was in all the papers."

At Needham Manor, I'd learned about his previous marriage, but not the circumstances surrounding his wife's death. Eager to learn more, I asked, "When was this?"

"About twelve years ago."

That explained why I hadn't heard about it at that time. "I would have been fourteen then. At that time, my only interests were my studies." Papa had been adamant about his daughters receiving the same education as his sons. Well, as much as could be managed. I was denied the privilege of enrolling at Oxford as that august university has not seen fit to admit women to its curriculum of study. "Papa hired the finest tutors for me."

"While my father insisted I make myself agreeable to marriage-inclined gentlemen of the nobility."

"At fourteen?"

Her mouth twisted with distaste. "Never too young to learn, as far as he was concerned. He didn't care if they were young and handsome or decrepit old prunes. All he concerned himself with was the size of their purses and how much they were willing to pay for my favors in their bed. As soon as I made my debut, Edmunds submitted the highest bid. He was desperate for an heir, and thought a young wife would provide that for him." She glanced down. "It didn't, but not for his lack of effort."

I squeezed her hand. "I'm sorry you had to suffer through that." Thankfully, I did not have to endure that fate. Papa had insisted on a debut season. But he'd left it up to me to decide who, and if, I wanted to marry. Even at eighteen years of age, I'd had no desire to put myself under a man's dominion.

Claire turned her attention back to the entrance. "Not every woman suffers in their marriage. The duke's, by all accounts, was a love match on both sides. They married before the season was over. He's still grieving for her, so much so he refuses to marry again. Many a single lady in this room would love to change his mind."

So ladies did know. They just sought to convince him to try again. "Why is he attending this ball, do you think?" Could he be in search of a new mistress as Claire claimed? Somehow, I doubted it.

She glanced off toward the receiving line once more. "I think he's here for political reasons. He's a leader at the House of Lords, you know. He might be trying to convince a few peers to vote for a measure he favors or vote against one he doesn't."

A gentleman I recognized suddenly emerged from the crowd. "Lady Rosalynd."

"Lord Selfgren." I plastered on a smile. "How pleasant to see you." Eight years ago, he'd asked Father for my hand in marriage. I'd turned him down, and he'd gone on to marry another lady. Sadly, she'd passed away a year ago.

"May I have the pleasure of this dance?" he asked.

The last thing I wished to do with the ballroom as crowded as it was. "I would prefer a promenade. It's such a crush," I said, nodding to the throng of dancers.

"As you wish. Shall we?" he asked, offering his arm.

As we made our way around the perimeter of the room, our conversation proceeded along the usual rules of etiquette. We both hoped we were in good health. I asked about his family. To my surprise, he talked about his children at some length. Clearly, they were very dear to him.

"Little Johnny is almost seven, and Isabelle is a very precocious five. She's already reading."

"How marvelous."

"The twins just turned two. They're coming along."

"Splendid."

After guiding us to a spot empty of guests, he drew our stroll to a halt and faced me. "How is your family faring?"

I shared general details about my sisters and brothers.

"And Rosehaven? Is he still deep in the weeds as it were?"

An odd way to refer to my brother's love of botany. "He is."

"A splendid hobby that. Is there a Lady Rosehaven on the horizon?"

"Not as far as I know. Cosmos is deeply devoted to his studies of flora." Where was he going with this discussion?

"You must desire to manage your own household rather than your brother's."

Ahh. It now became clear. He was looking for a mother for his children. But I would not do. "Actually, I'm quite pleased with my arrangement. Forgive me, Lord Selfgren, but I'm growing quite heated. Could I beg you to fetch me a glass of lemonade?"

His mouth turned down, no doubt with disappointment, as he likely desired to continue our discussion. Still, he offered a polite reply. "Of course, Lady Rosalynd." And, after a bow, off he went.

As soon as he was out of sight, I escaped into a corridor that ran alongside the ballroom. Thankfully, it was empty and, surprisingly, much cooler. There had to be a door or a window open to the elements somewhere close by. As I meandered down the hallway in search of the source, I heard male voices coming from one of the rooms. I would have continued with my exploration if not for the sudden mention of my name.

"Lady Rosalynd, Rosehaven's sister, submitted a petition to the House of Lords. She wants the legislation committee to introduce a measure to grant ladies the vote. She wrote it under the auspices of the Society for the Advancement of Women. Have you ever heard a sillier name?"

"Heard worse," a deep voice I recognized said, even as a chorus of laughter broke out among the gentlemen.

"Surely, you have no interest in introducing a bill to give women suffrage, Steele."

"I don't."

I gritted my teeth.

"Ladies should concern themselves with the begetting of children," the first male voice asserted. "After all, that's why we marry them. And leave the management of the country to us."

"Hear, hear!" another gentleman said.

"How did you dispose of the petition?" the Duke of Steele, he of the deep voice, asked.

"I tossed it into the fireplace and watched it burn."

As another round of laughter circled the group of men, my breath hitched. I'd labored on that proposal for hours only to have it laughed at and consigned to the flames. I was so angry I could barely breathe.

"You're awfully silent, Steele," the braggart said. "You don't agree with my disposition of the letter?"

"Lady Rosalynd will be expecting an answer."

"You handle it. After all, you're a member of the legislation committee as well. I'm off to the card room. Anyone care to join me in a game of whist?"

Every man seemed to agree with the suggestion. Only the Duke of Steele declined.

Their fading voices hinted at another exit from the room. Just as well. If they had come my way, I would not have been able to contain my fury. How dare they treat our petition so cavalierly?

"Lady Rosalynd! There you are! I've been searching for you." Lord Selfgren had found me. He was holding two glasses of lemonade and sporting a silly grin.

I couldn't inflict my ire on him. He had done nothing wrong. "I do apologize, Lord Selfgren. I needed the services of a maid in the withdrawing room. My gown had suffered a torn flounce."

"Ah, I see. Are you still eager for a lemonade? I fear it's grown lukewarm."

I forced a smile to my face. "No matter, sir. I thank you for it." I took the glass and drank half of it. Warm it may have been, but it did quench my thirst.

When the strains of a waltz reached us, Lord Selfgren's head snapped up. "I'm afraid I must leave you. I promised a lady this dance."

Thank goodness. I was in no mood to continue our inane conversation. Still, I had to be polite. "Don't think anything of it, milord. Thank you for fetching the drink. It was quite refreshing."

"Until we meet again, milady." He offered an elegant bow and, with a spritely step, returned to the ballroom in search of another candidate to mother his children. Whoever he chose would indeed be fortunate, as Lord Selfgren was not a bad sort. He was kind, held a title, and possessed a very comfortable fortune. But none of those attributes would tempt me to marry.

I dropped my now-empty glass on a tray strategically

located by a potted plant and walked toward the space where I'd left Claire. But I encountered her before I arrived.

"Where have you been?" she asked.

I pulled her aside. "You know how they say you shouldn't eavesdrop when someone mentions your name?"

"Because you won't hear a good thing about you?"

"Yes."

"Who? What?"

"A few so-called gentlemen in a room off the side corridor. I didn't mean to listen, but—"

Claire grabbed my arm. "Why, I'll be! He's walking toward us."

"Who?"

"The Duke of Steele."

Much too soon, he was in front of us. A tall, broad-shouldered presence who blocked everyone behind him from view. Everything about him was daunting, from his towering height to his commanding physique. Much as every other gentleman in the room, he was dressed in formal evening clothes. But while most other men's attire somehow seemed pedestrian, his were the epitome of sophistication and elegance. While I was busy taking his measure, he offered a very fine leg to my friend. "Lady Edmunds."

She curtsied in turn. "Your Grace."

Time seemed to stand still as his silver gaze found me. Unsettling and mesmerizing, it left me both strangely exposed and drawn to him. As it had done in the past.

"Lady Rosalynd," his deep voice sent shivers down my spine. After he bowed and I curtsied, he held out his hand. "Would you honor me with a dance?"

Not likely. "I'm afraid I'm—"

Digging an elbow into my side, Claire answered for me. "She'd be happy to."

I shot her an incendiary glance. But the truth of the matter was I had no recourse but to accept his offer, even as I wondered why he'd made it in the first place.

Unfortunately, the dance was a waltz, a particular aversion of mine. Not only that, I was roasting. "The ballroom is rather warm, Your Grace. Would you mind if we moved closer to the terrace? Our hostess seems to have thrown open the doors. It should provide cooler air."

"As you wish."

I rested my hand on the arm he extended, and together we made our way in that direction.

During our walk, we maintained silence. Seemingly, he'd reached the same conclusion I had. No sense talking when all around us, guests were practically shouting to make themselves heard. Once we arrived at a space that was blessedly devoid of people, he stopped and turned to me. "Will this do, Lady Rosalynd?"

"Yes, thank you." I gazed pointedly at him. "Why did you ask me to dance, Your Grace?"

He appeared to be momentarily taken aback by my question. Still, he answered me readily enough. "It is the thing one does at a ball, is it not?"

"And yet, I sense you have a specific purpose."

He offered a subdued, controlled upturn of the lips. Not the first time I'd seen that gesture on him. "I believe you overheard a conversation about the petition you submitted to the House of Lords."

"You're right. I did. How did you know?"

"Selfgren called out your name. Once your conversation with him ended, I followed you."

"For what reason? Surely not to claim a dance. You're

not in the market for a wife. And I wouldn't qualify as a mistress."

His silver gaze grew flinty. "You're angry."

"How very observant of you," I spat out through gritted teeth. "But you're wrong. I'm not angry. I'm furious. How dare you think women are too stupid to vote?"

"I did not say that."

"No, you didn't. But when another so-called gentleman espoused that view, you did not disagree."

"I'm depending on that gentleman's vote for a measure I favor. He would not vote my way if I contradicted his opinion in public." A logical, sound explanation, which I was not inclined to placidly accept.

"Fine. So what is your thinking about women's suffrage?"

"It won't happen. At least not in this century. Members of the House of Lords believe women lack the education to make informed decisions."

"And whose fault is that, I ask you, sir?" My voice rose with the anger and frustration I'd been feeling since I heard my petition had been so ignominiously tossed into the fire. "If gentlemen don't educate their daughters, our only recourse is to educate ourselves. Of course, many fathers would never allow that. As far as they're concerned, the only skills a lady needs are embroidery, playing the pianoforte, and dancing. Oh, and making herself agreeable to marriage-minded gentlemen who are only interested in one thing, providing them with a bloody heir."

He arched a brow. "Etiquette and comportment seemed to have gone missing from your curriculum, I see."

"As well as yours. A gentleman would not toss that insult to a lady's face."

"Rosalynd!" Grandmother's voice stopped me cold. Her

flushed face and snapping eyes spoke volumes about her state of mind. "What in heaven's name are you doing? You're making a spectacle of yourself," she hissed as she closed on me, heavily leaning on her cane.

Suddenly, I became aware that the music had stopped. Most of the guests around us stood open-mouthed, ogling the duke and me.

Grandmother curtsied to the duke, or tried to. Her creaking knees would not cooperate. "I beg your pardon, Your Grace."

"No need to, Lady Rosehaven." He bowed to both of us. "Your servant, ladies." And then he strode off through the path the throng made for him as if he were the Prince of Wales himself.

"Honestly." They should just drop to their knees and lick his boots.

Grandmother wrapped an arm around mine and hauled me off. For an elderly lady, she had a mighty strong grip.

"Where are we going, Grandmother?"

"We're leaving. Smile and nod. If not for yourself, for your sister."

I did as I was told, only to be met by a sea of frowns and snickers, with Claire the only friendly face. After collecting Chrissie, we walked out of the ballroom with our heads held high.

Only when we were ensconced in the Rosehaven carriage did Chrissie ask, "Why did we leave so early?" She was right. It wasn't even midnight. Balls usually lasted until three in the morning.

"Your sister decided to make a cake out of herself."

"What happened?" Chrissie asked, her eyes sparking with curiosity.

"I quarreled with the Duke of Steele in the ballroom in front of the entire assemblage."

"Why?"

"Because he's an ass."

Chrissie giggled. "Oh, my."

Grandmother stamped her cane on the carriage floor. "Young lady, your sister may have very well ruined your chances of making an advantageous match."

Chrissie hitched up her chin as she curled her arm around mine. "If a gentleman is so easily dissuaded against offering for me by a public quarrel, then I want no part of him."

I patted her hand. "Thank you, Chrissie. But Grandmother is right. I did make a spectacle of myself."

"If you did, you must have had a good reason."

I spilled the sorry tale of what I'd overheard and the quarrel in the ballroom with the duke.

"You'll need to apologize to him, Rosalynd," Grandmother said.

"I'll write him a note."

"A personal apology would be better."

"I don't see how that can be achieved. I can't very well visit him." Ladies of quality did not call upon gentlemen of the nobility. Not unless they wanted their reputations ruined.

She sighed. "I suppose a note will have to do."

Now all I had to do was find a way to apologize without revealing I wasn't the least bit sorry.

CHAPTER
THREE

A SURPRISE REQUEST

"You wished to see me, Cosmos?" My dear brother had requested my presence in his study. With its stacks of books, journals, plant specimens, and laboratory equipment, the room clearly branded him a scientist. So did the spectacles perched on his nose.

His coloring, on the other hand, identified him as a member of the Rosehaven brood. Our hair ran in all shades of red, from Chrissie's strawberry gold to Cosmo's dark burgundy and every other shade in between, including my own copper tresses, a feature I shared with our youngest sister.

"I hope I didn't interrupt a worthwhile endeavor," he said.

"Chrissie and I were taking stock of her wardrobe."

"Nothing important then." If the subject did not revolve around his beloved plants and flowers, Cosmos deemed the topic of no import.

I laughed. "Only if you don't deem the gown she will

wear for the Duchess of Comingford's ball important." One of the most important events of the season. Anyone who showed up in less than fashionable attire would be deemed not worth knowing.

His face fell. "I beg your pardon. I did not realize."

He was always so sweet about his contrition, I could never be angry at him. "Never mind. Why did you send for me?"

"Steele sent a note. He would like an audience with you. Odd that he asked for my permission." He gazed at me, a question in his eyes. "Do you know what that's about?"

"We enjoyed a ... conversation last night at Lady Cholmondley-Smith's ball. I raised a couple of points about women's education. More than likely, he wants to follow up on them." I wasn't lying. I had talked with him on that subject. True, it'd been an argument, but it did qualify as a conversation. It was strange that he was seeking an audience with me, however. Having sent him a note of apology this morning, I'd expected that to be the end of it. Apparently, the duke thought differently. If he thought I would offer more than I'd stated in my missive, he was sadly mistaken.

"I don't have to be present, do I?" Cosmos asked, an anxious tone in his voice. "Him being a duke and all."

That was the last thing I wanted. My disagreement with the duke was bound to come up during that conversation, something I was reluctant for Cosmos to know. I purposefully kept my brother ignorant of all the unpleasantries of life. Not only did they upset him, but he attempted to fix what was wrong in ways that made the situation worse. "No, Brother, you don't. It's bound to be a rather pedestrian conversation. May I read his note?"

"Of course." He handed it to me.

The message had been written on letterhead embossed with an escutcheon that depicted a blade at the top, a sword on the right, and a cannon on the left—the Steele coat of arms. Nothing less was to be expected from a duke whose ancestors were famous for fighting in numerous battles. Grateful kings had been so thankful for their efforts they'd awarded the family vast estates and increasingly more prestigious titles, culminating in the Steele dukedom.

It didn't take long for me to read Steele's note. As Cosmos had stated, he was seeking an audience with me, preferably today. He did not mention the reason for it.

"You could invite him to tea," Cosmos suggested.

"No!' I said a little too emphatically.

Cosmos' brows knitted. "Why not?"

Bother! He was growing suspicious. I had to convince him nothing was wrong before he stepped in to "solve" the problem. "It just ... it needs to be a private meeting." I grinned to make light of it. "You know how the children are. They'll be chattering nonstop. We'd never be able to discuss anything in their presence. We'll meet in the morning room. That way we won't be disturbed."

His wrinkled brow smoothed. "Whatever you think is best. Now I must be off. I have a lecture to attend."

Thank heaven. He needed to be away before Steele showed up. Otherwise, he might take it into his head to drop into our discussion. "On which topic, dear brother?"

"Foxglove's Medicinal Benefits."

That surprised me. "Isn't foxglove a poison?"

"It is, but as the lecture title indicates, it has health benefits too." He pointed to a plant in the corner that he had under glass. "I'm studying it at the moment."

"That's foxglove?" I asked in horror.

"Indeed, it is, dear sister."

"That plant shouldn't be here, Cosmos. You know how inquisitive Petunia is. And Fox is following in your footsteps. No telling what he might do."

"That's why I keep my study locked. Now, I really must leave. After you, Rosie." Once we walked out, he carefully locked the door behind us before making his way down the hallway.

Eager to study the duke's letter, I took it back to my room. The more I read it, the more concerned I became. What did the duke wish to discuss? Well, I wouldn't find out by standing here. I penned a quick note suggesting a meeting at three.

CHAPTER
FOUR

A MEETING WITH THE DUKE

I'd bathed, donned fresh clothes, and had my maid style my hair. If the duke was looking for a confrontation, I would meet him faultlessly attired and groomed. He would find no fault with me.

At the appointed hour, almost to the dot, our butler knocked on the morning room door. "His Grace the Duke of Steele, milady."

"Thank you, Honeycutt."

Steele strode into the morning room with the sure gait of a man who knew his worth in the world. He was dressed in unrelenting black, his favorite attire, the only spots of white his shirt and cravat. The strands of grey that streaked his black as sin mane, more obvious in the cold light of day than last night's candlelit ballroom, lent him a rather sinister air.

"Your Grace." I offered him my best curtsy.

He reciprocated in kind with an exquisite bow. "Lady Rosalynd. Thank you for seeing me."

"My pleasure." I wanted to say just the opposite, but I didn't want him to comment about my lack of manners as he had last night. I would play the perfect hostess, no matter how difficult it would prove to be. "I ordered tea." I pointed to the silver service on a low table. "Unless you wish for something stronger?"

"Tea will do." Taking a seat on the blue damask settee opposite the matching one I occupied, he asked, "Will Rosehaven be joining us?"

"My brother had a lecture to attend. He apologizes for his absence." Cosmos had done no such thing, mainly because it would never occur to him.

His brow knitted, as if he found my answer unacceptable. I did not have to wonder why. An unmarried lady meeting in private with a gentleman was simply not done. But it was what it was.

"Do you take sugar or milk?" I asked.

"Neither, thank you."

Having prepared the beverage to his preference, I handed him the cup and saucer. "If you're concerned about my lack of chaperone, don't be. I'm years past my debut season."

He frowned. "But you're still of marriageable age, and thus, in need of one."

I poured myself a cup before giving him a measured answer. "I have no plans to marry." As he well knew. I'd made that intent clear at Needham Manor.

"That's not the point. You can be ruined if anyone discovers we met in private."

"No one will. The only one who knows of our meeting is Cosmos, and he won't breathe a word."

He nodded toward the door. "Your butler knows."

"Honeycutt is the soul of discretion." I calmly took a sip

of tea while glancing directly at him. "You need not worry about your reputation, Your Grace."

His gaze bounced back to me. "It's yours I'm worried about, not mine."

"Are you inclined to ravish me then, Your Grace?"

His left brow arched. I'd surprised him. "Of course not."

"Well, there you are. I'm perfectly safe in your company."

For a few moments, his eyes focused intently on me as if he were trying to decipher a complex puzzle. "You're rather unusual. I should have remembered."

I bit back a grin. "Thank you, although I doubt you meant it as a compliment. Now, what did you wish to discuss?"

"I was dissatisfied with how things ended between us last night."

"Things did not end, Your Grace, because they never began."

"Be that as it may, you accused me of being less than a gentleman."

"I apologized. Didn't you get my note?"

"I did." His upper lip twitched, creating a lopsided grin. "Beautifully written as it was, I didn't get the feeling you were the least bit sorry."

"Oh, dear. I'll need to improve my groveling skills."

The quirk became more pronounced, transforming his face from cold and forbidding to something quite mesmerizing. Drat! I'd forgotten he possessed a sense of humor. I would need to beware. He was fascinating enough as it was. Thankfully, in the next instant, he became all business. "The reason I requested this meeting was because I wished to extend an olive branch."

That was the last thing I expected from him. "I'm listening."

"Lord Naughton disposed of your petition in a rather shabby manner."

"Shabby?" My ire rose hot and swift. "He tossed it into the fire like yesterday's refuse. I spent hours writing it. The least he could have done was write me a letter noting its disposition."

"I agree."

"Do you really?" I gazed at him, wondering what game he was playing.

"It would have been the proper thing to do. Your proposal deserved better. *You* deserved better. And that leads to the reason I'm here. Because he treated it in such a discourteous manner, I'm willing to espouse the petition by introducing it at our next Legislation Committee meeting. I will argue it should be considered by the full House of Lords."

To say he'd surprised me was an understatement. "I'm speechless, Your Grace. Thank you."

He sipped his tea before offering a response. "I said considered, not approved, which is what will most surely happen."

"You don't think it will be moved to the floor for discussion?"

"No, I don't. Many members of the House of Lords believe—"

"—that women lack the education to make informed decisions. You also hold that belief."

He nodded. "I do."

Anger threatened to rise once more, but I couldn't allow it full rein. He was extending a peace offering, after all. I would need to discuss the subject in a way he would understand. "Women lack education because they're not given the opportunity. While fathers of the nobility provide their sons with a first-rate education at Oxford and Cambridge, their daughters are only taught the social graces. It's no wonder they grow up ignorant of the world around them."

"And what do you propose be done? We can't force those universities to enroll women."

"Parliament can create schools of higher learning where women can study advanced subjects. They wouldn't have to be as prestigious as Oxford or Cambridge. They could be smaller ones, located around the country, that qualified females could attend."

"Such schools already exist, do they not? The Cheltenham Ladies' College and Roedean School, to name two."

"But only for those who can afford them, Your Grace. We need to provide for everyone, not just the privileged few."

"Even if Parliament was willing to create such schools, I doubt many ladies would enroll. Those who are unmarried need to work to earn a living. If married, they need to attend to their husband and children."

"The schools would only accept unmarried ladies. Full tuition as well as room and board would be offered."

"If such were the case, everyone would seek to attend."

"There would be a rigorous entrance exam, of course, which would include references from trusted sources. Only those who qualified would be allowed to enroll."

"And what would women do with that knowledge?"

Was he really that dense? "The same thing men do. They could become physicians, solicitors, scientists. There is no limit to what women can do. Half of our population is women, Your Grace. By denying them an education, Parliament is preventing progress."

The door suddenly crashed open. Just as the day before, Petunia burst into the room. "Are you coming to tea, Rosie?" She came to a screeching stop when she realized I was not alone. "Oh."

"Where are your manners, Petunia? You know you're supposed to knock."

She gazed down at the rug, a contrite expression on her face. "I'm sorry." A grin poked through.

She wasn't the least bit sorry, the little imp. I would need to have a serious discussion with her. But not at the moment.

"Your Grace, this is my scapegrace sister, Lady Petunia." I gazed at him, expecting a polite acknowledgement. But his eyes had widened as if a jolt of lightning had coursed through his veins, leaving him momentarily stunned. Was it shock or disapproval at Petunia's sudden entrance? He wouldn't have any children in his life, given his wife had died in childbirth during their first year of marriage. Maybe he expected Petunia to be a miniature adult, cognizant of all the strictures demanded of Victorian society. She tended to follow her own set of rules. At the moment, however, she would need to observe some of the customary ones. "Petunia, make your curtsy to the Duke of Steele."

"Milord." Her curtsy could not be faulted. It was perfection itself.

But there was one thing I had to correct. "It's Your Grace, not Milord."

"Why?" she asked, scratching her nose.

"Because dukes are addressed in that fashion."

"Why?"

"Because etiquette rules demand it. Now stop asking questions and return to the drawing room."

Her face fell. "You're not joining us for tea?"

"As you can see, I'm having a private conversation with His Grace. I'll be there by and by."

To my surprise, the duke came to his feet. "Actually, I'm afraid I must leave. I have an appointment at Westminster in half an hour. I'll notify you regarding the disposition of the matter we discussed. No need to ring for your butler. I can find my own way out. Your servant, ladies." He bowed, and in the next instance, was gone.

I stared at the space he'd occupied. How very odd. We'd been having a productive discussion. But as soon as Petunia barged into the room, his mood underwent a drastic change. He couldn't leave fast enough.

"You're not angry at me, Rosie?" Her lower lip was trembling, and her eyes were swimming with tears. This time, she was truly contrite.

"No, poppet. I'm not."

Quick as lightning, her mood changed. "Good, let's go have tea before Holly and Ivy gobble all the fairy cakes."

She curled her hand around mine as we made our way to the drawing room, but even as we did, I kept thinking about the duke's odd reaction to Petunia's entrance. What on earth could have caused it?

CHAPTER
FIVE

A DUKE PONDERS HIS ACTIONS

The walk across the square to Steele House would not take long. After all, Steele House was located directly opposite the Rosehaven residence. But needing time to think, I opted for a stroll around the Grosvenor Square perimeter.

The main thought that occupied my mind was the impetuousness of my actions. To start with, I'd sent a note to Rosehaven requesting an audience with Lady Rosalynd to discuss the disposition of her petition. That had been out of character. I hadn't committed the transgression; Naughton had. It would be up to him to apologize, not me. But after Lady Rosalynd's outburst at the ball, I felt the need to take on that responsibility. It should have been an easy thing to do. A quick apology and a quicker exit. But then I found myself volunteering to bring up the petition before the full legislation committee. I'd had no intention of doing such a thing before I entered the room. I hadn't even thought about it, if the truth be told. And yet the words had spilled out.

Why had I done it? The thing didn't have a prayer of making it to the floor of the House of Lords. Was it because I wanted to make amends for Naughton? Because I resented being branded as less than a gentleman? Or was it the spark of life—no, not a spark—the fire that blazed within Lady Rosalynd?

"Your Grace!" A loud female voice suddenly hailed me.

I gazed toward the voice's direction to find the Dowager Lady Throckmorton descending from her carriage. Much as I wished to avoid a woman who thrived on town gossip and destroying reputations, I couldn't do so. Good manners required a proper greeting. Putting thought to action, I doffed my top hat. "Lady Throckmorton."

"Fancy meeting you just as we arrive from the country." Her smile held the note of a cat who'd been presented with a dish of cream. She was pleased about our fortuitous encounter, unusually so. And that put me on alert.

"My good fortune. I hope you had a pleasant trip."

"It was tolerable. Train travel can be quite exhausting even in first class."

Behind her, a young woman descended from the carriage. A relation, going by her strong resemblance to the dowager. They both possessed dark curls with a widow's peak, brown eyes that slanted at the edges, and patrician noses.

"May I introduce my granddaughter, Lady Scarlet, Throckmorton's girl. She's making her debut this season."

Her glee at seeing me suddenly made sense. She was on the hunt for a husband for her granddaughter. And I was one of the most eligible gentlemen among the nobility. "A pleasure, Lady Scarlet." I bowed.

"Your Grace," the young woman curtsied as she blushed. She was quite lovely with her dark ringlets and shy smile. She would do well this season.

"Our arrival in town was a tad delayed due to unforeseen circumstances," Lady Throckmorton continued. "But we mean to make up for lost time. You should come over for a dish of tea. Are you free Tuesday?"

Her matchmaking tactics were blatantly obvious. I would have to disappoint her as I was unavailable for tea, not to mention marriage. "Afraid not, ma'am. A meeting at the House of Lords."

"All afternoon?"

"Unfortunately. We're reviewing our legislation agenda."

Her lips pinched with disapproval. "I suppose you must attend to your duties."

"Exactly so."

"The Walsh ball is next Thursday. I trust you will be attending."

That event was on my calendar as several members of the House of Lords would be in attendance. As I was seeking votes for a measure I favored, it would be a great opportunity to discuss it with them. "Yes, ma'am."

"Excellent." She became all smiles. "My granddaughter will save the first waltz for you."

"I'd be honored to, ma'am." It was only one dance. Afterward, I could avoid the damsel easily enough.

Eager to get away, I glanced toward the entrance to Steele House. But before I could put action to thought, a young sprig of fashion sprang down the Throckmortons' front steps. "Grandmama!"

"Rodney. How are you, my boy?" She greeted him with an honest smile while presenting her cheek for a kiss.

Having done so, Lord Rodney pouted. "Better now that you're here. It's been positively dreadful without your presence to brighten our dark world."

"You are the sweetest boy." She pinched her grandson's cheek before turning to me. "You know Steele, of course."

"Your Grace." The Throckmorton grandson was everything a young dandy should be. A blue fitted coat that flared out at the waist, matching trousers, and a silk brocade waistcoat patterned in blue flowers. A carefully tied cravat was tied in an intricate knot. A high collared, heavily starched shirt whose points were so sharp he'd surely injure himself if he moved his head too much. Last but not least, hair heavily pomaded to keep his pompadour in place.

"Lord Rodney," I murmured before turning back to Lady Throckmorton. "I'm afraid I must leave you, ma'am. Duty calls."

"Yes, of course. Don't forget about the waltz."

"I won't." Thankfully, Steele house was but a few doors down, far enough that the dowager wouldn't be visiting. Not that she would. Ladies, whether widowed, married, or single, didn't call on unmarried men. At least not on their own. If they did, tongues would most surely wag.

My butler must have been on the lookout as he opened the door as soon as I climbed the steps.

"Trying day, Your Grace?"

"Only the last few minutes." I handed him my hat, cape, and gloves. "Remind me again, Milford. Who is Lord Rodney in the Throckmorton lineage?" I didn't keep up with such things, but my butler knew every resident in Grosvenor Square and every family tree.

"Lord Throckmorton's second son." Throckmorton had inherited the marquisate a decade ago after his father passed on to his glory. A blustery sort, the current marquis spent most of his time at his gentleman's club playing cards and smoking cigars.

"Who's his heir?"

"Viscount Heywood, his oldest."

"And Lady Scarlet?"

"Lord Throckmorton's sole daughter."

So she would be a sister to Lord Rodney and Viscount Heywood. "Why is her grandmother sponsoring her debut rather than her own mother?" It hadn't been difficult to determine Lady Throckmorton's eagerness to push her granddaughter in my direction. She'd brought the young lady to town to find her a husband. I was a ducal widower in need of an heir. Ergo, I was at the top of her list.

"Lady Throckmorton is an invalid, Your Grace. She never leaves Throckmorton Manor."

"I see."

"If I may, your Grace. You have a visitor. Your brother, Lord Nicholas. I showed him to the drawing room."

"He's been watered and fed?"

Milford's lips quirked. "Yes, Your Grace."

I walked into the drawing room to find Nicky seated by a small table on which the tea service rested. Whatever had been on the plate in front of him, he'd devoured it as nothing was left.

"Nicky." I pointed to the empty plate. "I see you're eating me out of house and home."

"Not quite. I saved you a few crumbs." He came to his feet and embraced me. Five years younger than me, we shared the same physical traits. Whereas I was the responsible one, Nicky was the optimist, and our youngest brother, Philip, the rebel.

"To what do I owe the pleasure of your visit?" We were

not strangers by any means, as we enjoyed supper once a week. But it'd been only two days since the last one.

He flashed a grin full of mischief. "I come bearing news, Brother. Mother is back in town."

"Ah," I said. "I thought she wasn't due to return for another fortnight."

"She moved up the trip. Apparently, fashions have changed, and she needs an entirely new wardrobe before venturing into society."

"She's always loved fashion. I sense a lightening of my purse."

His brow wrinkled. "Why frown on something she truly enjoys? She had a difficult enough time with Father."

Our father had been a strict disciplinarian who heavily used his fists. If any of us committed the slightest infraction, he took the strap to us. I shielded my brothers as best I could. Unfortunately, I couldn't do as much for Mother, who was a regular victim of his drunken rages. He actually enjoyed beating her black and blue. And then one night, unable to bear her anguished cries any longer, I marched into their bedroom, ripped the strap from his hand, and used it on him. He never hurt her or my brothers again.

Not long after, he'd gone to the stables, ordered my favorite stallion saddled and ridden off drunk into the night. The next morning, we found him dead, his neck broken. My horse broken as well. I'd shot the stallion to stop his suffering.

"Forgive me, I didn't mean to criticize Mother. She deserves to enjoy what she can out of life."

"My apologies. I misunderstood." His impish grin returned. "That's not the only reason she returned. There's another."

"Oh?"

Nicky rocked back on his heels. Clearly, he was enjoying himself. "Mother intends to find you a wife this season. And she won't be fobbed off."

Not bloody likely. Approaching the sideboard, I poured myself a drink before turning back to Nicky. "A useless pursuit. She knows I don't intend to marry again." Once was more than enough. "Would you like a drink?"

"No, thank you. You need an heir, Warwick."

I sipped the liquor before clamping a hand on Nicky's shoulder. "That's what you're for, dear brother. The ladies seem to like you well enough."

In an instant, his grin vanished. "I don't think so."

"Something wrong?"

"I'm not in the market for a wife. Maybe Philip."

"No." I tossed back the rest of the whisky. "Not Philip."

"What's he done now?"

I told him.

"What do you intend to do about it?"

"Stop him from destroying himself. But it's damn hard."

"You are Steele to him."

That was my title, but Nicky's words conveyed something else. "What do you mean?"

"You have power over him, Warwick. Indeed, all of us, Mother, Philip, and me. Without you, we have nothing, as Father did not see it fit to bequeath us any funds, not even Mother. We are dependent on you for the roofs over our heads and every morsel we eat."

"I've never denied any of you."

"Indeed, you haven't. You've always been more than generous. Still, he resents it."

"And what am I supposed to do about it? As irresponsible as he is, I can't grant him a generous sum. He will squander it on women and ... other things."

"Talk to him."

"I have, Nicky. He won't listen."

"Then find another way."

I poured another generous splash of whiskey into my glass and gulped it down. "I'll see what I can do." Eager to change the subject, I asked, "Will you be at the Walsh ball?"

His smiling countenance disappeared, and his mood underwent a drastic change. "Yes, I'll be there." And then, without another word, he strode off.

That had been an odd reaction, especially coming from the brother who possessed the sunniest disposition of the three of us. Something was troubling him. Whatever it was, I would find out. He could never hide anything from me.

CHAPTER SIX

TEA REVELATIONS

On the best of days, afternoon tea at Rosehaven Mansion was a pleasant affair. The youngest conducted themselves like well-mannered children. No one spilled anything or slurped their Earl Grey like a walrus in a teacup. And everyone ate their pastries without causing a ruckus—even Petunia, who once declared, with great ceremony, that the last éclair was promised to her by fate and ought not to be contested.

Today was *not* one of those days.

I walked into the drawing room to find Holly and Ivy hoarding the tray of fairy cakes. Predictably, Petunia had taken objection and was trying to wrestle it away from them. Poor Chrissie was attempting to reason with the twins. But they turned up their noses at her and crammed more of the treat into their mouths. Fox, who'd been sent down from Eton after he'd fed an emetic to a group of bullies, causing them to vomit for hours on end, was staring morosely out the window. *That* was never a good sign. And Laurel, book in hand, had withdrawn to the farthest corner of the room, more than likely hoping the earth would swallow her quarreling siblings so she could read in peace.

Desperate times call for desperate measures.

I clapped my hands to get their attention. When that didn't work, I stomped my feet. It had the desired effect. All heads turned toward me. "Children. If you don't stop this arguing, you will all be vanished to your rooms with no supper, no books, and no dessert."

Laurel shot to her feet. "Why should I suffer? I'm not fighting over some silly fairy cakes."

Scrunching my brow, I folded my arms across my waist. "The punishment will apply equally to all."

She swallowed hard and threw herself back in her chair. "That's not fair."

"You're right. It isn't." I glared at Ivy, Holly, and Petunia. "Well, what do you have to say for yourselves?"

A red-faced Holly came upright. "Petunia commandeered the entire tray of fairy cakes. And she wouldn't share." With a triumphant grin, she said, "So Ivy and I took it from her."

"They ate most of them, Rosie," Petunia said, pouting. "There's almost none left for me."

There was only one solution to this problem. "Chrissie, please bring me the tray."

After a brief tussle, Holly and Ivy gave it up. As soon as Chrissie's back was turned, they stuck out their tongues at Petunia.

Once I had the tray in my possession, I handed it to the maid who was standing by the pastries table. "Please return it to the kitchen with my compliments to Cook. Tell her it's to be shared among the staff." Not that there were many left.

The maid curtsied. "Yes, milady."

As the maid made her way out the door, Petunia jumped to her feet, her eyes filled with tears. "No!"

"Sit down, Petunia."

It was a sad little imp who retook her seat.

"Since you cannot behave yourselves, no fairy cakes will be served for the next seven days. They will return only when you demonstrate proper decorum. Is that clear?"

Dead silence met my pronouncement.

"I can't hear you!"

A chorus of "Yes, ma'am," and "Yes, Rosie" circled the room.

"Now, one at a time, starting with Chrissie and proceeding in descending order of birth, you will each serve yourselves one sweet from the pastries table. You will then sit and eat it like the ladies and gentleman I know you are. There will be no talking, no pelting each other with food, no sly glances. If I detect the slightest infraction of these rules, you will all be vanished to your rooms. Nod if you understand."

They all nodded.

"Chrissie, if you will, why don't you start us off?"

As she passed me, her lips quivered with mirth. But sticking to the rule I'd just laid out, she didn't say a word. One by one, her siblings followed equally silent. Once they'd helped themselves, they returned to their seats and proceeded to eat quietly.

Into this ocean of calm walked our butler, Honeycutt. "You have a visitor, ma'am. Lady Walsh."

I turned to find my cousin walking toward me. "Julia,

how pleasant to see you." Embracing her, I kissed her cheek.

"Rosalynd," her smile was more sad than happy, which unfortunately was often the case these days. She'd made her debut the same year I had. Unlike me, though, she'd been eager to marry a titled lord. But lacking a large dowry, she believed her chances were slim of capturing the attention of a gentleman of noble birth.

That season, however, Lord Walsh, a widower of one year, had been on the hunt for a wife. His son, who suffered from a weak disposition, was not expected to make old bones. So Lord Walsh was eager to marry a young lady who would provide him with the spare he desperately needed. In Julia, he'd found the perfect candidate. "I hope you don't mind my dropping in."

"Of course not. You're welcomed any time." I led her to a settee where we could enjoy a comfortable coze. "Would you like some tea?"

"Yes, sugar only, please."

I nodded to the maid in charge of the tea service, who prepared a cup to Julia's preference and served it to her.

"How are the ball preparations coming along?" In years past, her celebrations had been perfectly splendid, but this season I'd sensed a lack of excitement in her. Maybe she'd grown tired of all the work that went into them.

Still, she answered pleasantly enough. "Very well. I just hope it goes off without a hitch." She put a palm to her stomach as if her anxiety was making itself felt in that region.

I pressed her hand. "I'm sure it will be perfectly splendid."

"It's just nerves, I know." She removed her gloves so she

could drink her tea. That's when I noticed the bruises on her arms.

"What happened?" I whispered, pointing to her forearm.

"It's nothing. Walsh was a bit too ... amorous, that's all." Her voice descended into a whisper.

What kind of lovemaking inflicted such bruises on a woman's fair skin? "Really?"

"He likes to hold me down when we ..." she murmured without finishing the thought.

I hitched a brow. It wasn't the first time I'd seen marks on her arms. And her shoulders as well. One time, I'd spotted the imprint of a man's hand around her throat. Today she was wearing a high-neck gown. Could she be hiding bruises there as well? "He should take more care with you."

Her lips twisted. "You wouldn't know, Rosalynd, since you're not married. Marital relations can be quite physical."

To the point of inflicting damage? I yearned to ask. But now was neither the time nor the place to hold such a discussion. It would have to wait until after the ball. But afterward, I would most surely bring it up. I feared what her husband would do to her.

After his first wife died from a fall down the stairs, a rumor had spread that he'd caused her death. Nothing had ever been proven. Indeed, no charges had ever been brought. But in the years Julia had been married, she hadn't been able to conceive a child. And Walsh was growing desperate for another son.

His son Charles had married against the advice of his physician, who'd warned him marital relations would stress his heart. Predictably, Lord Walsh had grown even more frantic. If Charles met his demise, the title and the

Walsh estate would go to Walsh's nephew, something Walsh desperately wanted to avoid. He might very well be thinking of doing away with Julia so he could marry a third time and get the spare he so ardently desired.

"Let us not quarrel, Rosalynd," Julia suggested. "Can we talk about happier things?"

"Yes, of course. What would you like to discuss?"

"The ball. I was wondering about—"

She proceeded to ask my opinion about details which I deemed rather minor. But it did make her happy to discuss such things with me. So I didn't hesitate to offer my advice. By the time she left, she seemed to be in a better frame of mind. I was glad our conversation had done her some good. But after the ball, we'd be having a serious discussion about her husband's treatment of her. Such behavior could not continue.

CHAPTER
SEVEN

A MOTHER'S CONCERN

I was seated at my desk drafting the speech I planned to present before the legislation committee, espousing Lady Rosalynd's petition for women's suffrage. Given the original had been consigned to the fire, I had no knowledge of the language she had employed. But I knew the committee. The best way to couch the plea would be to explain how it would benefit them. I doubted it would pass muster, which meant it would not make it to the full House of Lords. But I had to try. I had promised Lady Rosalynd.

Suddenly, a presence made itself known. My butler was standing inside my study door. "Begging your pardon, Your Grace. I did knock. You have a visitor."

I'd been so deep in my thoughts, I'd failed to hear it. "Who?" I asked, somewhat annoyed.

Milford cleared his throat. "Her Grace, the Duchess of Steele."

He'd barely breathed the words when Mother drifted

into the room. "Warwick, sorry to barge in like this. I hope I'm not disturbing you."

I rounded the desk and kissed her cheek. "Not at all." Taking a step back, I gazed at her. "You are looking well." Whenever we met, which was not as often as either of us desired, I was reminded of how beautiful she was. Her hair had turned silver, of course, but her ice blue eyes still sparkled with life, and she fairly vibrated with vitality. Age had neither withered her nor dimmed her spirits.

A soft smile bloomed across her lips. "Thank you for saying that, my boy. It does take longer to make oneself presentable these days."

"You are much more than presentable, Mother."

"Flatterer." Her lips turned up at the corners. A sign she truly enjoyed the compliment.

I glanced at my butler, who was still standing at the door, a warm expression on his face. He'd always had a soft spot for Mother. "Tea, please, Milford." Mother was a stickler for observing the niceties. She enjoyed her refreshments whenever she came to visit.

"Of course, Your Grace."

"Shall we take a seat?" I pointed to her favorite settee.

As she arranged herself on the seat, she glanced around my study. A smile and a nod signaled her approval. "This room. You haven't changed a thing."

"Why should I? I like it the way it is." I took a seat on the sofa opposite her.

"Even when there's a decided feminine flair to it?" Many years ago, she'd had the settee and sofa upholstered in her favorite shade of blue to match the color of her eyes.

"Even so. It reminds me of you."

Her face flushed from my praise. But then she quickly moved on. "Well, at least the books are of your choosing.

Your father had no interest in reading. And the bones of the room are good."

"Yes, they are." All around, the walls bore shelves of finely crafted wood, each one filled with leather-bound volumes. History, philosophy, law, and politics lined the shelves, spines pressed soldier-straight. The scent of old books and pipe tobacco lingered in the air, blending with the faint aroma of sandalwood from the furniture polish. Above them, the paneled walls rose to a coffered ceiling, the carved detailing there recalling the long line of ancestral distinction they bore.

A knock on the door preceded the entrance of a maid with the tea service. After she placed it on the low table between the sofa and the settee, Mother poured tea and served biscuits for us both.

"Did you receive my note?" I asked before taking a sip of the fragrant tea. "I planned to see you this afternoon." First thing this morning, I'd sent a missive asking for permission to call on her. No answer had been returned, but then I hadn't expected one until after noon. It was just about that time now.

"I did. But I have an appointment with the modiste this afternoon. So I thought I'd come to you." She barely sipped her tea before she said, "We have something serious to discuss."

Knowing what the topic would be, I rested the cup on the table between us. "Yes, Nicky told me."

"It's time you marry, Warwick." Mother's voice, usually so composed and measured, now held a quiet plea. She sat before me, her posture stiff.

"You know my feelings on the subject, Mother," I said, holding her gaze. "I don't intend to do so again." I tried to keep my tone steady, but bitterness threatened to seep through. My marriage had left me more scarred than I cared to admit.

Her lips tightened, but her eyes shimmered with concern. "I know how much you suffered, dear boy. Any man would have shattered under such torment—watching someone he loved fade away like that." Her voice wavered as she leaned forward. "But medicine has advanced in the last decade, Warwick. Physicians now specialize in obstetrics. They can prevent such a horror from befalling you again. The likelihood of a miscarriage is so very slight."

Memories surged unbidden—the panic, the screams, the helplessness. The scent of blood and the hollow ache of loss. "But not impossible," I said, my voice no more than a rasp. "I refuse to risk putting another woman through that kind of suffering. I will not gamble with a life, remote as the chance may be."

Mother's cheeks hollowed, and for a moment, I saw the pain my stance caused her. I knew she worried for our legacy as much as my happiness.

"And how will the Steele line continue?" she asked, more softly now, as though the question itself wounded her.

I forced a half-smile, bitter and resigned. "I prefer to leave that chore to Nicky," I managed, trying to inject a note of wry amusement. But the truth hung heavy in the air.

She shook her head, something almost like pity twisting her features. "I wouldn't count on him if I were you." The words fell heavily, lingering like the memory of old grief. It seemed we were both trapped—in her case by the fate of our family, in mine by the haunting shadows of a past I could never quite outrun.

"Why not?" I demanded, my voice sharper than I intended.

She drew in a measured breath and looked away, as if ashamed to speak aloud. "He's ... involved with a married woman," she said quietly, her voice weighted with sadness. "He won't be considering a wife of his own anytime soon."

My stomach twisted. This explained Nicky's fierce reaction earlier, the tension that crackled in his words. "Who?" I forced the question through gritted teeth.

"I don't tell tales out of school," she said, eyes lowered. "You'll have to speak to Nicky himself if you want a name."

I surged to my feet, unable to remain still, not with fury and disbelief coursing through my veins. Pacing the length of the study, I demanded, "Why would he do something so reckless? It would surely bring a scandal to our family's good name."

Mother's voice softened, as though she pitied both my anger and my brother's plight. "He doesn't see it as wrong, my dear. He's blinded by love. He truly believes it will all work out somehow."

"Work out?" I hissed through clenched teeth. "He can't possibly believe the woman would seek a divorce and run off with him. We cannot allow this. The notoriety would stain the Steele name beyond repair."

Mother's hand trembled, causing her teacup to clatter in its saucer. "The lady's husband is a brute," she said, her voice catching as though it pained her to admit. "He beats her ... regularly." Her face contorted with old sorrow, and for a moment, I feared she'd be lost to memories best left buried. "If your father hadn't—"

I bit back a groan of regret. "Please, Mother," I said, softening my voice. "Don't torment yourself with the past. I didn't intend to stir those old ghosts."

She pressed her lips together and gave a tight nod, as if

banishing unwelcome recollections. "You're right," she said, her tone strained but determined.

My thoughts swirled with anger. "A brute who harms his wife. There must be something I can do."

"No," Mother said firmly, something fierce and protective sparking in her eyes. "Nicky would never forgive you if you intervened. The husband already suspects an affair. If you involve yourself, you'll prove him right. God knows what he might do to that poor woman in retaliation."

I drew back, my hands fisting at my sides. "How long has this been going on?" I asked, stunned by the lengths my brother might have taken without my notice. "He's only been in town for a month."

Mother's gaze met mine, filled with a sorrow that went bone-deep. "It started last year," she said softly, and in that moment, I felt the crushing weight of all I didn't know. How had I missed that?

"If that's the case," I said, my voice low and taut, "the affair won't last long. I'll make certain he understands what a grievous error he's making."

Hope flickered in her eyes as she leaned forward. "You'll speak with him, then?" Her voice trembled slightly, as though my mere words could lift the weight pressing against her heart.

"Of course." I clenched my jaw. "Did you doubt I would?" I leveled her with a steady look, trying to reassure. But would I be able to sway my brother's dangerous course? At the very least, I had to try.

"Thank you," she whispered, relief softening her features. Then she broached her favorite topic once more. "As for the other matter…"

I let out a harsh breath, my patience stretched thin. She would not rest until I gave her the answer she craved, no matter how firmly I refused. Gritting my teeth, I crossed to the sideboard, seized the decanter, and poured a generous measure of whiskey. The amber liquid caught the light as I swallowed it down in one long, desperate gulp.

"There is a candidate, Warwick," she said, her tone gentling as if that would soften my resolve. "You've already made her acquaintance."

I forced a thin, humorless smile. "I've met countless women, Mother."

She pressed on, undeterred. "Lady Rosalynd Rosehaven. You know her brother, the Earl of Rosehaven."

I closed my eyes briefly, then opened them, determined to steer this conversation away from marriage. "Yes, I'm aware." Desperate for a distraction, I asked, "What happened to her parents?"

She paused, voice quietening as if to honor the dead. "They perished six years ago in a terrible carriage accident. They were returning from a social event when the bridge they were crossing collapsed beneath them. The next day, they were found, clinging to each other."

I grimaced, the tragedy weighing heavier than I cared to admit. "At least they died together," I said, the bitterness in my tone betraying what I truly felt. No one deserved such a fate.

"That calamity left their children orphaned," Mother continued softly. "Lady Rosalynd, barely eighteen, gave up any thought of marriage. Instead, she remained at their Yorkshire estate to raise her younger siblings. Her first season was her last."

"She's content with her life," I said, trying to sound detached.

"How can you be so certain?" Mother asked.

I kept my gaze fixed on a point beyond her shoulder. "She told me she doesn't wish to marry."

"You broached the subject with her?"

"No. She volunteered it on her own."

"Her grandmother, the dowager, said as much," Mother replied, a trace of disappointment lacing her words. "A shame, really. She'd make a splendid mother."

I stiffened at that gleam in Mother's eyes. I knew that look too well. It was the same one she'd directed at me before my betrothal. "She won't abandon her siblings, and I have no intention of marrying." My words were flint and stone, striking sparks between us.

"There's her sister," Mother pressed, voice smooth as velvet. "She's making her debut this season. Malleable. Fertile stock. There are nine children in that family. Can you imagine? She'd give you heirs."

Pressing my lips together, I shut my eyes again. "No," I said, final and firm.

Mother sighed, rising to her feet in a graceful flutter of silks. "Just think about it. That's all I ask." Her voice had lost none of its persistence, yet it softened with maternal affection. "I'm off to the modiste."

For a moment, I hesitated before kissing her cheek. Despite the vexing nature of our talk, I could not deny her the small comfort of that familiar gesture. "Thank you for coming," I managed, though annoyance still simmered beneath my cordial tone.

She studied me, her forehead creasing with a small line of worry. "You are looking after your brothers, aren't you, Warwick?"

I drew back and straightened my shoulders. "Do not fret, Mother," I said quietly. "I am keeping an eye on them." Even if neither wished me to do so.

CHAPTER
EIGHT

LADY WALSH'S BALL

The ballroom at Walsh House glittered with a thousand points of light. Candlelit chandeliers hung from the lofty ceiling and refracted off gilded mirrors, bathing the elegantly dressed guests in a warm, shifting glow. Every person of note in London society seemed to have converged here. Jewels winked at throats and wrists, silks whispered along parquet floors, and a hum of polite laughter and music wove through the crowd.

I scarcely wanted to be here. I preferred my study—its quiet order, its refuge of papers and inkwells—to the chaotic brightness of a crowded ball. But duty demanded I attend. There were several important gentlemen who had yet to commit their votes to my pending measure in the House of Lords. With Parliament in session, I needed every edge. If it took a few waltzes and some flattery delivered through a forced smile, so be it.

At some point, I would have to ask Lady Throckmorton's granddaughter to dance. But not now. Not just yet.

As a string quartet in the gallery began a lively tune, couples drifted to the center of the floor. I kept to the perimeter, nursing a glass of champagne I had no real interest in drinking. My eyes scanned the crowd, searching for those particular gentlemen, noting their absence yet again. If they did not appear soon, I would have attended this charade in vain.

And then, almost as if it sought her out, my gaze found Lady Rosalynd. She was calmly observing the festivities with a detached air while standing near a marble pillar. Her gown, a soft dove-gray silk, was unadorned except for tiny seed pearls at the neckline, elegant but understated. She was not the sort to clamor for attention. Well, except when her ire was raised. She got it nonetheless. Both her beauty and bright copper hair couldn't be missed. As usual, some of her curls had escaped the—no doubt—painstakingly sculptured arrangement. Much like the lady herself, they would not be tamed.

With the gentlemen I sought nowhere in sight, and my patience already frayed by the endless clamor of small talk, I found myself strolling across the floor toward her. It was unlike me, but something in her repose, so out of step with the frantic gaiety around us, drew me on.

When I reached her side, she offered a slight curtsy, just on the side of proper etiquette. Probably in case someone was watching. And somebody always was.

"Good evening, Lady Rosalynd," I said, keeping my tone cordial. "I trust you're enjoying your cousin's ball?"

Her lips curved, though not in a smile of delight. More like a private amusement. "I find it as diverting as any crowded, noisy event might be, Your Grace."

I inclined my head in acknowledgment. "High praise indeed."

She said nothing, only looked over the dancers, as if trying to recall why people chose to whirl about to violin music.

"I trust you did not attend such an event unchaperoned."

A small smile acknowledged our conversation of two days ago. "No, Your Grace, my grandmother is here, along with my sister. She's making her debut this season."

"Yes, I remember." We'd both been invited to Christmas festivities at Needham Manor in Yorkshire. But when a priceless necklace had been stolen, an investigation into its disappearance had taken up most of our time. I wondered what she would say if I asked her to dance. She'd once refused the same offer.

I offered my hand. "I believe the set is just beginning. Will you do me the honor?"

Her eyes narrowed. Exactly as I expected, she replied, "I would rather not, Your Grace."

My hand remained extended. "Alas, if you do not, you risk insulting your own cousin. It is her ball, after all. Think of the talk if you refuse the Duke of Steele so publicly." The last time we'd met, our public disagreement had caused a stir. I doubted she wished to do so again.

Her gaze flicked from my hand to the crowd around us. Clearly, others were watching. Backing away now would not prove to her advantage, or her cousin's. Finally, her delicate, gloved fingers touched mine.

"Very well," she said, voice cold as a winter morning. "One dance, Your Grace. Let's make it count."

We moved onto the floor and took our places among the other couples. The music began—some old-fashioned dance, the steps of which had been drilled into me from my youth. Polite, controlled, we moved in graceful motion. From a distance, we must have appeared the very picture of harmony. Up close, our words were anything but.

"I wonder," she began softly when we came together, her voice low enough that no one else could overhear, "if you derive pleasure from cornering ladies into compliance. Is that the secret to your famed political success, Your Grace?"

I nearly missed a step. That amused me, I could not lie. "No," I returned, keeping my tone mild. "I find it much easier to maneuver gentlemen in the House of Lords than to force an unwilling lady to dance."

"How fortunate that I am here to pose a challenge then," she said dryly. "And what is it you hope to gain by this dance?"

I tilted my head. "I hoped for three minutes of civilized conversation. One can grow weary of endless chatter on fashion and scandal. I thought you might offer something more substantial."

"Is that supposed to flatter me, Your Grace? You drag me onto the ballroom floor to avoid boredom?"

"Perhaps," I said, feeling a strange thrill at sparring with her. Most women would have simpered or at least pretended that faint praise was welcome. Not her. She parried and countered like a skilled duelist. "Maybe I sought your company because I find you intriguing."

Her elegant brow arched, more than likely with disbelief. "Let us say I remain unconvinced."

Once more, the swirl of dancers drew us apart, spinning her into a different pairing. I caught sight of her through the shifting crowd—her gaze distant, her posture stiff—and when the music guided us back into each other's arms,

I immediately sensed a change. The brittle sharpness in her eyes had softened, and something—regret, perhaps—shadowed her fine features.

She lifted her chin slightly, and I could almost feel the tension vibrating within her. "I apologize, Your Grace," she said, her voice quiet yet laden with sincerity.

My brow creased. Only moments before, she'd met every word of mine with resistance, each phrase with an unsheathed edge of steel. "For what reason?" I asked, confused by this sudden reversal.

"I was rude," she replied, refusing to meet my gaze. "Argumentative, while you've done nothing but show politeness. I was taking out my frustrations on you."

Her confession pricked at something inside me, stirring a curious sympathy. We moved through the next steps, skirts swishing and slippered feet gliding over polished floors. "Does something weigh on you?" I asked, as questions tugged at my mind.

A flicker of distress passed over her face. "Yes," she admitted, her voice low. "My cousin's husband, Lord Walsh, has not shown his face at his own ball. Julia is utterly mortified. This was to be their grand evening, and he leaves her to greet a sea of guests alone."

The tension mounted between us as her words pressed on the very air we breathed. "Perhaps he is merely delayed," I offered, trying to reassure her, though I found it difficult to believe a gentleman would be so careless.

Her lips parted, and she swallowed hard, a tremor flashing through her. "If he was in fact delayed, he should have sent a note, a messenger—anything to explain. But there's been no word." She glanced toward the entrance of the ballroom, where her cousin, Lady Walsh, had stood earlier, bright and proud in her finery. Now, that familiar figure was gone. The empty space where she should have been felt like a dark void, absorbing the laughter and chatter into uneasy silence.

The violins continued their lilting melody, but Lady Rosalynd did not appear to hear them. Her gaze drifted restlessly among the guests, searching for answers that did not reveal themselves. "It's well past ten," she murmured, her voice threaded with growing worry. "He knew this night was special, how important it was to her."

In that moment, I understood. Her earlier barbs had been shields, masking an anxiety she did not want to claim as her own. She did not fear for just the evening's success, but for the well-being of someone she cared about. Someone who'd been left alone in a spotlight that should have been shared. And so, as we continued to dance, our steps now slower, more deliberate, I held her troubled gaze and sought to find the right words to ease her doubt.

But before I could do so, a piercing scream sliced through the music. Instantly, the dancers halted. Heads turned toward the double doors leading out into the corridor. Instinct and duty propelled me forward, even as I released Lady Rosalynd's hand. She refused to be abandoned, however, and followed me as I left the dance floor.

"I advise you to remain behind," I said over my shoulder to her as we moved. "This may not be suitable for—"

She shot me a sharp look. "If something terrible has happened, I will not cower behind potted palms."

We emerged into the corridor just as Lady Walsh herself stumbled into the ballroom. The hostess's beautiful gown hung awkwardly, and her face was white as a sheet. A hush fell over the guests like a heavy curtain.

"He's dead," Lady Walsh gasped, her voice cracking. "He's dead!"

A shocked murmur spread through the guests. My brother Nicky, standing not far from the center of the crowd, caught Lady Walsh's eye. When her gaze latched onto him for a fleeting instant, my stomach clenched with sick certainty.

Lady Walsh was the married woman entangled with my brother.

I had hoped to speak to him tonight and dissuade him from this madness, I had not imagined it would come to light in such a dreadful manner.

Rushing forward, I pushed past a cluster of horrified onlookers, reaching Lady Walsh just before her knees gave out. She fell against me, her trembling fingers clutching at my lapels. The scent of jasmine clung faintly to her hair. She tried to speak, but her words broke off into sobs.

"Steady," I said, supporting her weight. Over her shoulder, I caught Nicky's eye. His face was pale with shock. He started to move forward, but I shook my head. Thankfully, he acknowledged my command and made no further move toward her. His clothing was just as disheveled as hers. Had they been engaged in something untoward?

In the next instant, others pressed in—Lady Rosalynd among them, her expression grave and eyes full of concern. As I felt the weight of the entire ballroom's attention, whispers started at the edges, hissing possibilities and suspicions into the charged air.

"Who's dead, Julia?" Lady Rosalynd asked softly as she knelt next to her cousin.

Lady Walsh's voice emerged again, thin and fractured. As her lips trembled, I leaned closer, straining to catch her words. "Walsh," she managed, her voice barely above a whisper, "someone murdered him."

CHAPTER
NINE

THE TRUTH COMES OUT

Stepping out of Julia's bedchamber, I paused in the deserted upper corridor of Walsh House, my heart still thudding from the night's horrors. Barely an hour ago, the ballroom had swirled with silk and chatter. Now, the air smelled of sputtering candle wax and bitter endings. My cousin's glittering ball had ended in tragedy.

I leaned against the paneled wall, forcing my breath to steady. No use collapsing now. The terrible words replayed in my mind—He's dead!—and with them, the image of Julia crumpling into the Duke of Steele's arms, pale as a ghost and twice as broken.

Walsh had been found in Spitalfields, of all places. An area he'd have avoided like the plague on any ordinary evening, much less the night of his own grand ball. Now he lay dead, murdered, while Julia, his wife, hovered between consciousness and despair.

I swallowed the knot rising in my throat. Julia rested behind that closed door, attended by her maid and physician. But no physician could stitch her life back together. Not after this.

A shadow shifted nearby, and I looked up to find Steele lingering in the corridor, silent and immovable as a sentry. Given his earlier duties—summoning the doctor, carrying Julia upstairs—I had assumed he'd gone. Yet there he stood, as if some invisible tether kept him rooted here.

And he wasn't alone.

Chief Inspector Dodson, Scotland Yard's representative of grim efficiency, loitered at the end of the hallway. His eyes gleamed with calculation, taking stock of every word, every flicker of emotion. Some history existed between him and Steele. They watched each other like duelists waiting for the signal to draw.

I took a measure of comfort in the fact that Lord Nicholas, Steele's brother, had left the house. Sensible, really. After Julia's collapse, the rumor mill had ignited. His lingering presence would only have fanned the flames.

Still, I couldn't shake what I'd seen—the furtive glances, the concerned hovering. I'd been too wrapped up in Chrissie's debut to notice before. Was there truly something between Nicky and Julia? The thought gnawed at me, but now was hardly the time to chase shadows. Julia needed me to be strong.

I stepped closer to Steele, lowering my voice. "Your Grace, the physician has asked that Julia not be disturbed. She needs rest, not interrogation."

His steady, gray eyes met mine. "She will not be questioned tonight. You have my word."

I inclined my head, grateful for the reassurance. If only I could banish the other threat lingering at the end of the corridor.

Dodson had sidled closer, drawn by our whispers. His presence slithered across my skin like a cold draft.

"Chief Inspector," I said, polite but firm, "the doctor has made it clear Lady Walsh must rest. Whatever questions you have must wait."

Dodson's smile didn't reach his eyes. "I understand, Lady Rosalynd. But I have a duty to fulfill. Lord Walsh was found murdered in Spitalfields. I intend to discover why. With your permission, I shall inspect his study, speak to the staff. Perhaps by then Lady Walsh will feel strong enough to assist us."

"You may search his study and question the servants," I said crisply. "But Julia is not to be disturbed. Doctor's orders."

Before Dodson could press further, Steele stepped forward, a wall of black evening clothes and iron will. "Lady Walsh will not be distressed any further tonight," he said, voice brooking no argument. "You may return tomorrow, Inspector."

Dodson's jaw tightened, but he tipped his hat in grudging concession. "Very well. But I will return at first light."

I didn't doubt it. Men like Dodson thrived on blood in the water.

Once he disappeared down the staircase, silence reclaimed the corridor. I let out the breath I didn't realize I'd been holding.

Steele turned to me, weariness etched into his handsome features. "I'm sorry you had to witness this."

I managed a smile. Wan, but sincere. "We came expecting music and dancing. Not ..." I faltered, unwilling to finish the thought.

He nodded grimly. "No one could have foreseen this."

For a moment, we simply stood there, two reluctant soldiers thrown into the chaos of someone else's war.

"I'm concerned for your cousin," he added, then hesitated. "And for you."

"For me?" I blinked, startled.

"You're remarkably composed, considering the circumstances."

I flushed, recalling our prior, less-than-civil exchange on the dance floor. "One has little choice but to remain calm. Julia needs me more than I need indulgence in my own emotions."

Something like approval flickered in his gaze. "She's fortunate to have you."

The words warmed me, despite the grimness of the hour.

Still, my thoughts twisted back to the rumors. If Dodson caught the scent of anything untoward between Julia and Lord Nicholas, he would pursue it without mercy. I stole a glance at Julia's door, closed tight against a merciless world.

Poor Julia. She had tried so hard to do everything right—to be a good wife, a proper lady. Now she stood on the edge of scandal, teetering on a precipice she might never escape.

I drew a slow breath. "I should stay the night."

Steele didn't hesitate. "Of course."

"I must write a note to my brother. Would you deliver it to him?"

He simply nodded.

I quickly penned the missive in Julia's morning room, informing Cosmos where I would be and requesting that my maid, Tilly, arrive with fresh clothes in the morning. I couldn't very well remain in my ball gown. After handing it to Steele, I said, "Please impress upon Cosmos that this is urgent. He can be somewhat preoccupied."

That earned the ghost of a real smile from him, something that lightened the heavy gloom.

The physician emerged then, reporting that Julia was sleeping and should not be disturbed. After a few murmured reassurances, he, too, departed, leaving the house to its uneasy silence.

We descended the grand staircase together, Steele and I. The butler waited by the door, Steele's cape and hat in hand.

"Is Inspector Dodson still here?" Steele asked.

"In Lord Walsh's study, Your Grace," the butler murmured.

"See that he does not disturb Lady Walsh."

"Of course, Your Grace."

Steele turned back to me, his cape now draped over his shoulders. "If you need anything—anything at all—send word."

I nodded. "Thank you."

And then he was gone, swallowed by the night.

The housekeeper showed me to a hastily prepared bedchamber. Nothing grand, but it was clean, the sheets scented faintly of lavender, and someone had thoughtfully laid out a nightgown. I thanked her and made sure she knew no one was to disturb Julia unless absolutely necessary.

After a maid helped me out of my ball gown, I slipped beneath the covers, grateful I was alone. But sleep did not come easily. Somewhere in London, Lord Walsh's murderer walked free. Somewhere, the next revelation waited to shatter what remained of our fragile peace.

I vowed, right there and then, that I would not allow Julia to face it alone.

Not while there was breath left in my body.

CHAPTER TEN

A SCANDAL BREWING

I rose at dawn, though calling it sleep would have been generous. I'd spent most of the night staring at the ceiling, watching the shadows creep and shift, while the terrible events of the evening replayed themselves like a grim pantomime.

Tilly arrived promptly at eight with a set of fresh clothes. She found me already bathed and pacing. It took only a few minutes for her to wrestle me into a suitable gown—an achievement, considering I could hardly stand still.

She had just fastened the final buttons when raised voices shattered the early quiet.

"Oh, miss!" Tilly gasped, her reflection in the mirror wide-eyed with alarm.

"I must go!" I wrenched free.

"Wait, milady, just one more—"

I was already halfway to the door, propriety trailing in my wake.

I followed the shouting to Julia's morning room, stopping short at the sight that greeted me.

Charles Walsh, pale and wiry by nature, was now flushed red with fury, hands clenched at his sides as he spat venom at Julia.

"You take me for a fool?" he shouted, voice cracking. "A child, to be lied to at every turn? I see it clearly—you and your precious Nicky Thornburn conspired to rid yourselves of my father."

The accusation struck like a slap. For one awful moment, I stood frozen, stunned that anyone—least of all Charles—could accuse Julia of murder. His face, twisted with rage and grief, held no hint of doubt.

"Lower your voice, Charles," came a calmer tone behind him. Edwin Heller, Charles's cousin and seemingly peacemaker, stepped forward, his hand resting gently on Charles's shoulder. "You must calm yourself," he said, voice placating.

"Don't patronize me!" Charles snarled, though he didn't shake him off. "I will not be silent while my father's killer stands there feigning grief!" He thrust a trembling finger toward Julia.

Julia rose slowly to her feet, her hands shaking, her voice low but fierce. "You speak as if you never knew me at all. Your father's death wounds me deeply. I would never harm him or you."

Her words barely touched Charles. His laugh was a bitter, broken sound. "You call it foolishness? I think not. I've seen the way you and Thornburn look at each other. You never loved my father. You never loved me. You used us both for convenience. And now that he's dead, you expect sympathy?"

Julia's face, always so composed, crumpled slightly. But then, she drew herself up with the last shreds of dignity.

"I was faithful," she said, voice trembling but unyielding. "I gave everything I had to this family. I may not have given him a child while he was alive," she paused, her hand fluttering over her abdomen, "but now, by the grace of God, I carry one."

The room went deathly still.

Good heavens! Julia was increasing.

Charles's face contorted with fury. "You're with child?" he spat. "I refuse to believe it's my father's. Everyone knows about your association with Thornburn. How convenient that after years of barrenness, you suddenly find yourself expecting."

The accusation sliced through the air like a blade. This had gone too far. I stepped forward, inserting myself between them.

"Charles," I said, keeping my voice even, "please. We are all grieving. Let cooler heads prevail."

He turned his haunted eyes toward me. "Lady Rosalynd," he rasped. "Forgive me that you must witness such ugliness. But I cannot, will not, watch my father's murderer wear a widow's weeds without speaking the truth."

Before Julia could reply, Charles stormed from the room, the door slamming hard enough to rattle the windows. Edwin threw me a helpless look, then hurried after him.

Julia collapsed onto a chaise, burying her face in her hands.

I approached slowly, kneeling beside her. "Julia," I said gently, "are you all right?"

A foolish question. Of course, she wasn't.

She lifted her tear-streaked face. "I loved him, Rosalynd," she whispered. "I loved my husband. We had our trials. What marriage does not? But I never betrayed him. And now ... now I'm left with vile accusations and nothing to defend myself but my word."

I sat beside her, unsure which hurt more: hearing her pain, or realizing that no matter what I believed, the world would believe what it wanted.

After a moment, I asked cautiously, "Charles mentioned Nicky Thornburn. He said there was an attachment between you."

Julia's eyes widened, mortification and indignation warring across her face. "We are friends," she said fiercely. "Nothing more. I found him agreeable, yes. But I *never* betrayed my marriage vows."

Her words rang with conviction. But still, I recalled the way she and Nicky had looked at each other. Friendship? Perhaps. But friendship does not burn quite so brightly in the eyes.

"And yet," I said delicately, "after years of marriage, you are now increasing."

Color crept up Julia's neck. "It is a miracle," she whispered. "A miracle I never thought I'd know. Think what you will, Rosalynd, but trust me. This child I carry is my husband's."

Trust. Such a simple word. Such a heavy burden.

I squeezed her trembling hands. "Charles believes what he wants to believe. But we ..." I steadied my voice. "We will uncover the truth."

She nodded, grateful tears slipping free.

But in my heart, doubts gnawed at the edges. If society turned against Julia, they would turn against Nicky too.

And if Inspector Dodson had even an inkling of these rumors ...

I came to my feet. "Julia, I must go for a short time. You are to rest. No visitors, no callers."

"There will be callers," she said miserably. "They'll come sniffing for gossip like vultures."

"Let them peck elsewhere. I'll leave orders. No one is to be admitted."

I rang for her maid, issued strict instructions, and told the butler the same.

Only when I was certain Julia would be kept safe did I allow a footman to hail a hackney.

The drive to Steele House didn't take long. But even so, my mind churned the whole way.

Upon my arrival, Steele's butler ushered me into a stately sitting room. Steele did not keep me waiting long. He entered looking immaculate, controlled, and ... faintly wary.

"Lady Rosalynd," he said. "I expected a note, but not you in person. Has something happened?"

I rose. "Indeed, it has."

I told him about Charles's accusations, Julia's pregnancy, and the ugly web of suspicion tightening around our families.

His jaw tightened. "Nicky would never seduce a married woman," he said flatly.

"Perhaps not," I said. "But rumor cares little for truth."

Steele raked a hand through his dark hair. "This will spread."

"It already has," I said grimly. "And unless we act, it will consume them both."

He paced a few steps, thinking. When he turned back,

the steel in his expression matched his name. "We must take matters into our own hands."

I stared. "You mean investigate Walsh's murder?"

"Exactly."

For a moment, I could only blink. An investigation would mire us in a scandal. It was madness to involve ourselves in such an endeavor.

And yet.

"If we leave it to Dodson," Steele continued, "they'll be railroaded before the week is out. He cares for expediency, not truth."

"You know him?" I asked.

"All too well," Steele said grimly. "Several years ago, he was placed in charge of an embezzlement investigation. All evidence pointed to a young accountant, someone I knew. He was innocent. I was sure of it. But that didn't stop Dodson from clapping him in irons. By the time I discovered the true thief, the young gentleman was dead. Devastated by the shame the accusation brought to his family, he hanged himself."

"Oh, dear heaven. I'm so sorry."

"I took steps to have Dodson demoted. At the hearing, I argued that he should have conducted a more thorough investigation. But it proved to no avail. He was allowed to keep his rank, as there had been more than enough evidence to charge the accountant. The thing of it was if Dodson had been more diligent, he would have realized the documents had been forged by the young accountant's superior. But with Scotland Yard resources stretched as thin as they were, there was no time, or inclination, to do so."

"Dodson strikes me as a man who wants a quick solution to this murder."

"He is. And Lady Walsh and my brother are easy targets."

A sense of dread roiled through me. "We must be cautious," I said slowly. "If word spreads that we are interfering, it could look like we are trying to hide their guilt. We might hurt more than help."

"That is a risk," he allowed. "But consider the alternative. If we do nothing, the law may very well claim them both, whether they are guilty or not. We must not let that happen."

By the time he finished, my resolve had hardened into iron. "You're right. We must do this," I said. "For Julia. And for your brother."

He gave a firm nod of approval. "We'll need to keep in close contact so we can compare notes as needed. There is much to be examined. For starters, I need to find out where Nicky was that night. He arrived late at the ball."

"And we'll need to find out what Walsh was doing in Spitalfields."

He flicked a hand in dismissal. "He was visiting his mistress."

"What?"

"I managed to pry that information out of Dodson while you were attending to your cousin. Apparently, Walsh had a twice-weekly rendezvous with her."

"The dastard! How dare he?"

He glanced toward me. "Did your cousin know?"

"Of course not. She would have mentioned it."

"Would she?" His hard stare questioned.

"Maybe not," I conceded. I would need to find out.

"Find out what she knows about Walsh's dealings. What acquaintances did he have? Did she hear anything that would provide a clue? Once you've talked to her, we can arrange a meeting."

A thought occurred to me. "How do we do that without attracting attention? We'll open ourselves to gossip if we spend any time alone. We have enough trouble with the rumors swirling around Julia and Lord Nicholas."

A faint smile curved Steele's lips. "This is London society, Lady Rosalynd. People talk if a lady takes a stroll without her chaperone. But don't worry. I'll arrange for a private meeting place. You won't be caught out."

"It's not me I worry about, but Chrissie. This is her debut season. It would be ruined if I embroiled myself in a scandal."

"It'll be a place no one knows in an area no one is likely to visit. I'll send a note to Rosehaven House as soon as I've made the arrangements. Is that agreeable to you?"

"It has to be. There really is no other choice. Julia and I grew up together. If there is any chance that she is innocent, I must do all in my power to prove it."

"I feel the same way about Nicky. He may be a fool at times, but he is still my family." Taking a deep breath, he said, "We shall work together, in secret, and unravel this to the best of our abilities."

"Agreed," I said.

As I rose to leave, I met Steele's eyes. For the first time, I felt no distrust or wariness between us, but a shared and solemn vow.

We would find the truth.

No matter the cost.

CHAPTER ELEVEN

AN UNPLEASANT SURPRISE

Having spent longer with Steele than I intended, I rushed back to Walsh House, all the time praying nothing alarming had occurred. I stepped out of the hackney with an air of weary determination, brushing off the chill that clung to my traveling cloak.

The grand façade of Walsh House loomed before me, its stately windows glinting under the overcast afternoon sky. I had scarcely crossed the threshold when the butler, a usually unflappable man, approached me with an urgency that sent a ripple of unease down my spine.

"Milady," he murmured. "Inspector Dodson is here. He is speaking with Lady Julia in the drawing room."

My breath hitched. Unfortunately, my prayers had not been answered.

Without waiting for another word, I strode through the halls, my heels clicking against the polished marble. As I reached the drawing room, my grip tightened around the folds of my skirts. The deep timbre of Inspector Dodson's voice carried through the heavy doors.

"Are you expecting a child, Lady Walsh?"

My pulse quickened with indignation. How dare he ask such a personal question? I threw open the doors, my voice cutting through the tense silence. "Lady Walsh will not answer that."

Inspector Dodson turned, a slow, amused smirk curling at the corners of his mouth. He was a tall, hawkish man with an unsettling gaze that belied his polite demeanor.

"Lady Rosalynd," he drawled, inclining his head. "A pleasure."

I ignored his false pleasantries and stepped protectively toward my cousin. Julia sat stiff-backed on the settee, her gloved hands knotted together in her lap. Her pallor was even more pronounced than the last time I saw her.

"I am entitled to ask questions of her," Dodson said.

"Not without her solicitor present," I declared firmly.

Dodson's smirk widened. "Then I will expect to see her at Scotland Yard. Do let me know when she's ready to be brought in for formal questioning."

Julia let out a strangled gasp, her composure crumbling. The moment the inspector strode from the room, she dissolved into tears.

I was at my cousin's side in an instant, wrapping an arm around her shoulders. "Do not distress yourself, dearest. We will handle this."

Before Julia could respond, voices echoed from the entryway. A footman's muffled protest preceded the arrival of an unwished-for visitor—Lord Nicholas, Steele's brother.

His sudden appearance startled us both. He entered hastily, his dark hair disheveled and his expression tense with worry. His eyes immediately found Julia, and without hesitation, he crossed the room to kneel beside her settee. "Julia, my God," he murmured urgently, his gaze searching her face. "Are you all right?"

Julia's breath hitched softly, and her eyes welled with tears at his evident concern.

"Lord Nicholas, you shouldn't be here," I said in a no-nonsense tone.

He glanced apologetically at me. "Forgive me, Lady Rosalynd. I realize I'm intruding, but I couldn't stay away. The rumors ... Julia's distress. I had to know she was safe."

My voice grew stern. "Did Inspector Dodson see you?"

"Regrettably, yes," Nicky admitted. "I was just arriving when he was descending the front steps."

I slowly shook my head. Nothing worse than a fool in love. Did he even begin to realize what he'd done? "Your presence here will only fuel his suspicions. He already believes that you and Julia planned Lord Walsh's murder."

"That's absurd!" Lord Nicholas exclaimed, rushing to his feet, anguish plain in his voice. His fingers tightened on Julia's hand. "I could never ... Julia would never—"

"Nevertheless," I interrupted gently, "perception matters, Lord Nicholas. You must go."

Julia's eyes widened in alarm. "No! Rosalynd, please—"

"Julia," Lord Nicholas whispered tenderly, his thumb brushing gently over her knuckles, "Lady Rosalynd is right. I mustn't place you at further risk."

Julia turned pleading eyes toward him. "But if you leave now, they'll think—"

"They already think," I interjected. "Your innocence will speak louder if you remain apart."

Lord Nicholas drew a deep breath, torn by his conflicting emotions. "If there's anything I can do—"

"There isn't," I said, a note of finality in my voice. "Julia's safety and yours depends on discretion. Please, do as I say."

Julia, at last, lowered her eyes in reluctant acceptance. "Go," she whispered hoarsely, withdrawing her hand slowly from his. "For now."

He rose stiffly, his eyes lingering on Julia with undisguised anguish. "If you need me, send word immediately."

Once he had departed, an uncomfortable silence settled over the room. Julia's expression had hardened slightly, a quiet resentment flickering in her eyes. "You should leave too, Rosalynd," she said abruptly. "I can handle things from here."

She was lashing out at me because I'd banished Lord Nicholas. But it was something that needed to be done for her own good. "Very well. I shall do as you wish. At least allow me to contact Steele about arranging a solicitor."

Julia sighed heavily, her shoulders slumping with fatigue. "Yes. I would appreciate it if he could do that."

"I'll send him a note as soon as I arrive home."

"Thank you, Rosalynd." Her voice hadn't entirely thawed, but it had warmed. "I really do appreciate your kindness."

"You're welcome. If you need anything," I said, my words almost an echo of Lord Nicholas's.

"I'll send for you."

I stood slowly, my gaze lingering on Julia's weary face. Our bond, so strong only yesterday, now hung by a thread of wary distance. As the drawing room door closed softly behind me, I paused, uncertain and anxious about what the future would hold—for Julia, for Lord Nicholas, indeed, for all of us.

CHAPTER
TWELVE

STEELE VISITS HIS BROTHER

The note arrived with all the urgency of a war dispatch. Brought by one of Lady Walsh's footmen, according to Milford. I wasn't expecting it, not when I'd talked to Lady Rosalynd a bare hour ago. Something must have occurred at Walsh House. I tore open the envelope to find two paragraphs filling the space in a handwriting I recognized.

Upon my arrival at Walsh House, I found Dodson questioning Julia. I gave him his walking papers before too much damage was done. He wants to question her at Scotland Yard, so she'll need a solicitor. Can you please arrange for one?

Of course, I could. Hanover came to mind. Not only did he have a deep knowledge of the law, but he was trustworthy, discreet, and fiercely loyal to his clients. But Lady Rosalynd's note did not end with that request.

As Dodson was leaving, Lord Nicholas arrived. There's no doubt Dodson saw him.

The bloody fool!

I asked him to leave as his presence would do Julia no good. Nor himself, if I may add. I am returning to Rosehaven House. You may contact me there.

Lady Rosalynd did not explain the reason for her sudden departure from her cousin's home. But I could well imagine its impetus. Lady Walsh had objected to Lady Rosalynd asking Nicky to leave. An idiotic move on her part. Lady Rosalynd's presence would have protected her against accusations of improper behavior with my brother.

"Is there an answer, Your Grace?" Milford asked.

I shook my head. "No. But I will need a footman to carry a note to the City." That's where Hanover's chambers were located.

"Of course, Your Grace."

As Milford turned to leave, I said, "And order my carriage. I need to visit Lord Nicholas." And ring a peal over his head.

Milford simply nodded.

It took no time to pen the letter to Hanover. After explaining in detail what was needed, I asked him to contact me tomorrow. Once that was done, I made my way to the entrance hall where I handed the sealed letter to Milford. Within moments, I was on my way to Piccadilly.

Nicky's quarters were located in The Albany—a bastion of bachelorhood and discretion. It loomed before me as my carriage rolled to a stop. Alighting swiftly, I strode through the grand entrance without hesitation.

Save for the faint strains of music from a neighboring suite, Nicky's quarters were quiet. When no one answered my firm knock, I used my key and pushed open the door. Inside, the scent of brandy hung thick in the air. The source of it was my brother, sprawled on an armchair in the sitting room, a half-empty glass dangling from his fingertips.

His eyes, unfocused yet alert, landed on me with mild surprise. "Warwick," he drawled, tipping his glass in my direction. "What a rare pleasure."

"You're drunk," I noted flatly, stepping inside.

"Observant as ever," Nicky replied, swirling the amber liquid. "Did you come to lecture me?"

I ignored the bait and went straight to the point. "Did you visit Lady Walsh?"

"Yes."

"Are you in love with her?"

Nicky stiffened, the amusement in his expression fading. He set his glass down with deliberate care. "What of it?"

My pulse ticked faster. "Then it's true."

"It doesn't matter," he said curtly. "Nothing has happened between us."

I studied him, searching for any flicker of dishonesty. "Tell me about your encounters with her."

He exhaled, rubbing a hand over his face. "We talk. That's all we do. In ballrooms, at the theater, in public, always surrounded by half of London's elite. We laugh, we exchange barbs, but never—" his voice hardened "—never anything more."

I crossed my arms, unwilling to relent. "And yet, society has taken note of your affections."

Nicky scoffed. "As if society needs an excuse to talk."

"You should have exercised more caution. She's a married woman. Or rather was."

"And you should exercise less control!" Nicky's voice rose with sudden fury. "You act as though you dictate all outcomes, but not this time. Not with me."

I narrowed my eyes, as the tension built between us.

"This is not about control. It is about consequences. Where were you last night before your arrival at the ball?"

Nicky stood abruptly, the glass falling from his fingertips, the amber liquid spilling over the rug. "You think I murdered Walsh?"

"Of course not. But Dodson already suspects. He will ask, Nicky. You must have an alibi. Where the devil were you?"

"Get out."

I held his gaze, my own anger simmering beneath the surface. But there was nothing more to be done now, not while he was in this drunken state.

Without another word, I turned and strode out, the weight of the conversation pressing heavily upon me. It was only after I climbed back in my carriage, I could admit the truth. I'd handled that rather badly.

The carriage ride back to Grosvenor Square was a quiet one, though my mind was anything but still. Nicky's defiance still echoed in my ears, his anger, his indignation. It was a rare thing to see my brother so affected.

Unsettled as I was, I should have returned home so I could get back my bearings. But I needed to discuss what had just happened with someone. Not Mother. I didn't want to inflict that pain on her. The last thing she wanted to hear was that Nicky had taken to the bottle. It would bring back horrendous memories of our father when he'd taken out his drunken rages on her. The only other logical person was Lady Rosalynd. She had to have returned home by now.

After descending from the carriage in front of my residence, I made my way to Rosehaven House. It was not a long walk—just across Grosvenor Square. I was frostily received by their butler. No wonder, I'd arrived in all my dirt. I hadn't even stopped to shave. Pursing his lips, he stepped aside to allow me entry.

"I'd like to see Lady Rosalynd."

"Is she expecting Your Grace?"

"No."

"Very well. If you would follow me."

I thought he'd show me to the sitting room where we'd met before. But to my surprise, I soon found myself outside what turned out to be the drawing room. As the doors opened, the scent of tea and freshly baked goods filled the air. The Rosehaven clan had gathered for tea. It appeared to be a rather harmonious scene. The well-behaved children were quietly enjoying their refreshments and treats.

"His Grace, the Duke of Steele, milady," the butler said while tossing a rather superior air toward me.

Well, that would teach me to show up uninvited and unshaven.

"Your Grace," Lady Rosalynd gracefully rose to her feet and curtsied. "What a pleasant surprise!"

It was nothing of the kind. We'd agreed to behave circumspectly. And yet, here I was, tossing all discretion to the wind.

"Lady Rosalynd." I bowed. "My apologies for arriving without an invitation. I thought it vital to discuss a recent turn of events."

Thankfully, she didn't question my statement. Just the opposite, she answered me warmly. "Yes, of course. May I suggest we enjoy our tea first? I hope you don't mind. Having missed my luncheon, I'm feeling rather peckish."

"No, of course not." What else could I say?

Once I took a seat and was presented with a cup of tea, I found several pairs of eyes staring at me.

"You know Cosmos." She pointed to her brother.

"Yes, of course."

"Steele," Cosmos murmured through a mouthful of scone.

"But you haven't met the rest of my family."

"I haven't had the pleasure, no."

"Chrissie, come and make your curtsy to His Grace."

A young woman, her hair the color of rose gold, came up and curtsied.

"My sister, Chrysanthemum," Rosalynd explained, "We call her Chrissie. She's making her debut this season."

Coming to my feet, I bowed. "I'm honored to make your acquaintance, Lady Chrysanthemum."

"Your Grace." Lady Chrysanthemum offered a graceful curtsy before returning to her seat.

Lady Rosalynd then motioned forward a younger version of herself. "This is Laurel. She's never to be found without a book, as you can see."

Indeed, one dangled from her hand. "Lady Laurel."

Laurel murmured something I didn't quite catch. Clearly, she resented the intrusion into her reading time.

"The twins, Holly and Ivy. Born on Christmas Day."

"How do you do, Your Grace?" They spoke in unison while bending their knees. From the hoydenish light in their eyes, I guessed they were mischief makers.

"Fox, please come forward to be presented to the duke." Once he'd done so, she introduced him. "Fox is the youngest male member of our family."

"Lord Fox. The one who loves poisonous plants, I've heard."

"Not only those, Your Grace. I also enjoy the carnivorous ones. They can be quite—"

"Thank you, Fox," Lady Rosalynd said, "you can discuss those another day."

Fox returned to the window, his tail tucked firmly behind his legs. Poor lad. Odd that he was in London. He should have been at Eton or Harrow.

"And last but not least—Petunia."

My breath caught once more. "Lady Petunia."

"How do you do?"

"Your Grace, poppet. Remember?"

"I can count to one hundred," Petunia said. "How high can you count, Your Grace?"

"I haven't really thought about it."

"Do you like fairy cakes?"

"I ... suppose?" What the devil were fairy cakes?

Her nose wrinkled with disapproval. "You suppose? You either love them or not. I love them." She flashed a grin that was missing two teeth. "Do you have any children?"

My heart stopped. "No. I don't."

"You're being impertinent, Petunia. Come sit by me." Grabbing Petunia's arm, Lady Chrysanthemum dragged her away.

"But I—"

"Here, have a fairy cake." Lady Chrysanthemum shoved a cake in the little girl's mouth.

That didn't deter Lady Petunia, however. Once she finished her treat, she continued to speak. "Chrissie is making her debut this season. She's been presented to the king and queen."

"That's excellent."

"She sings and dances beautifully. And she knows how to play the pianoforte. She'll make an excellent wife. Are you in the market for a wife, Your Grace?"

Lady Chrysanthemum choked on her scone. Holly and Ivy snickered. Laurel ignored the entire thing as her nose was firmly stuck to her book. Equally oblivious, Fox continued to stare out the window.

"No. I am not, Lady Petunia."

Her lip curled. "A shame."

"If your hunger has been satisfied, Your Grace," Lady Rosalynd said, "let us move our discussion to the morning room. We should be able to enjoy a private conversation there."

Hard to have satisfied my hunger as I hadn't had the chance to eat so much as a crumb.

CHAPTER
THIRTEEN

A STRATEGY SESSION

As soon as the door to the morning room clicked shut, I turned to face Steele. "I must apologize for Petunia. She's precocious beyond her years. Growing up surrounded by older siblings with no sense of discretion has left its mark."

A wry smile played at the corner of his mouth, though his eyes studied me more intently than I liked. "No need to apologize. But I confess, I'm intrigued. Petunia seemed rather determined to recommend Lady Chrysanthemum as a potential bride, yet ... " His gaze lingered, uncomfortably penetrating. "You seem the far more logical choice."

My breath caught. Still, he was owed an explanation. "Petunia is well acquainted with my views on marriage."

"That you never intend to enter into that state," he finished, his voice softer now.

"Precisely." The word was a shield. "Chrissie, on the other hand, is quite candid about her desire to wed. And Your Grace is a widower—"

"—so Petunia was playing matchmaker and praising her sister's charms to an eligible duke?" His eyes danced with holy amusement.

"Yes," I said, taking a seat on the settee. "I hope you weren't offended. She's rather taken with you."

"She barely knows me."

"Children don't always need time," I replied, my voice suddenly quieter. "Petunia sees people as they are. Last year, a gentleman took an interest in Chrissie at the village fair. Since he came from a perfectly respectable family, I invited him to a picnic. But Petunia disliked him immediately."

A shadow flickered across Steele's features. "Why?"

"She wouldn't say at first. Only that he was 'wrong.' I dismissed it as childish nonsense until word spread that he'd assaulted a village girl, ruining her. His family banished him to the West Indies before charges could be brought."

His expression hardened. "That doesn't solve anything. It just shifts the rot."

"True." Bitterness slipped into my tone. "But he didn't escape punishment. Last I heard, he was laboring on a sugar plantation. A far cry from society balls and cricket matches."

There was a beat of silence before I gestured to the chair he'd sat in earlier. "Please, Your Grace. Take a seat."

He didn't. Instead, he moved to the fireplace to stand with his back to me, tension coiling in every line of his form.

I watched him carefully. Something was definitely troubling him. "Perhaps we might speak of the reason you came."

He exhaled harshly. "I sent word to George Hanover.

He's acted as my solicitor before. I've asked him to meet with me tomorrow to discuss Julia's defense."

"Has he agreed?"

"He will."

I arched a brow. "You sound quite sure."

"No one says no to me, Lady Rosalynd."

He said it without arrogance—only weary certainty, as if he bore the weight of always being obeyed.

"Even so, he might have prior commitments. A meeting with a client, perhaps."

"If he does, he'll arrange it for another time." Steele raked a hand through his hair, the movement jagged with frustration. "After sending the letter to Hanover, I went to see Nicky."

I flinched inwardly. "And how did it go?"

His jaw clenched. "About as well as you might expect."

I didn't speak at once. The silence stretched, as he paced like a storm bottled inside four walls. When I finally spoke, my voice was gentle. "Would you like something to drink?"

"I don't need more bloody tea," he snapped, then instantly looked away, penitent. "Begging your pardon."

"Something stronger, then." I crossed to the bell and gave it a firm tug.

Honeycutt appeared a moment later, calm and imperturbable as always. "Milady?"

"His Grace would like a … whiskey?" I directed the question at Steele, who gave a terse nod.

Honeycutt inclined his head and vanished.

When I turned back, Steele was still standing. I narrowed my eyes. "Please, Your Grace. If you don't sit, I'll develop an awful crick in my neck."

A reluctant smile ghosted across his lips. "Forgive me,"

he murmured, and at last lowered himself onto the settee across from mine.

Honeycutt returned with a decanter and a glass. After pouring a generous measure, I handed the glass to Steele, who downed the liquor in a single swallow.

"Better?" I asked softly.

He didn't speak for a moment. Then: "Much." He leaned forward, elbows on his knees, hands gripping the glass. His hair was mussed now, the edges of his composure fraying.

"You've had a difficult day."

He gave a bitter laugh. "That's an understatement."

"Would you like to talk about it?"

"No. I would not."

I leaned back, my voice steady. "Very well. Then let's discuss how to proceed with the investigation."

He looked up, grateful for the return to process. "I'll start with Walsh's club. There's always gossip in those walls—someone may have seen or heard something. You should handle the distaff side."

"Women's gossip, you mean?" I asked with a sly smile.

He returned it. "Precisely. An afternoon tea or maybe a visit to the modiste. Gabrielle's is a fashionable haunt for the ladies, I'm told."

"You're familiar with Gabrielle's?"

"My mother visits there often," he said. "She never tires of new gowns."

I nodded, filing the detail away. "What else?"

"You'll need to return to your cousin's house. Ask if she heard or noticed anything. Anything at all."

"You don't believe it was a simple robbery?"

"No." He leaned back, eyes fixed on mine. "His wallet was untouched. His watch, his sapphire pin—still on his person."

"Perhaps there wasn't time?"

"There was. The body wasn't discovered for the space of an hour."

"How do you know?"

"Dodson. He shared that much with me. The officer who patrols that patch swore that Walsh was not there during his earlier round. Tellingly, no alarm was raised. Whoever struck the deadly blow did it boldly, efficiently."

A chill slithered down my spine. "You think someone hired a killer."

"The facts speak for themselves."

I would need to fashion an excuse for returning to Walsh House. After all, Julia had asked me to leave. But it was something that needed to be done. If the murderer had been known to Walsh or Julia, a member of her staff might provide clues as to who it could have been.

A heavy silence settled between us, thick with things left unsaid. Then I asked, more softly than intended, "Have you considered a place we might meet again?"

He nodded, his gaze shadowed. "I own a house in Chelsea. Quiet. Discreet. No one of consequence will be watching."

I rose and fetched paper and pencil, the scratch of graphite loud in the stillness. He scribbled the address with quick, deliberate strokes and handed it to me. His fingers brushed mine—a fleeting touch, no more than a breath—but it sparked through me like fire catching on dry paper. We both felt it, and neither spoke of it.

"I'll go to Walsh's club tomorrow evening," he said, voice returning to its usual clipped control. "You should visit your cousin in the morning. Early afternoon at the latest."

"When should we reconvene?"

"Our next meeting can't happen for several days. There's the inquest to get through. It won't take place before Monday."

"And the reading of Walsh's will follows afterward. Not the same day, of course. So Tuesday? Wednesday?"

"I'll send word. What time suits you best?"

"Not the morning. Early afternoon. Say two?"

He inclined his head. "Two it is, at the address I provided."

"And Mr. Hanover?"

"I'll see that he visits Julia tomorrow."

I nodded, then paused—something twisting low in my chest. "Do you think your brother will stay away from her?"

A muscle ticked in his jaw. "If he doesn't," he said, each word like a stone dropped into still water, "I'll make certain he regrets it."

I didn't doubt him for a moment.

Heaven help anyone—friend, brother, or foe—who stood in his way.

CHAPTER
FOURTEEN

BROKEN FORTUNES, BROKEN MEN

The following evening, I arrived at White's a little after eight. Prime time, when the club's walls practically hummed with power, ambition, and secrets better left unspoken.

Though the full evening bustle had not yet peaked, a fair number of gentlemen were already cloistered inside, dining, wagering, and murmuring over their brandy glasses. The air was thick with cigar smoke, the sharp tang of leather polish, and the musty weight of old sins. White's was not a place one visited for virtue. It was a hunting ground for advantage, where truth could be cornered and dragged into the light. If a man had the nerve.

I handed my greatcoat and gloves to the attendant and moved through the polished mahogany halls, acknowledging a few acquaintances with the barest of nods. My title opened every door here, and tonight I intended to make full use of it.

The gaming salon buzzed with muted energy under

flickering gaslights, the ancestral portraits glaring down in silent judgment. Here, fortunes were made and broken. Sometimes in a single hand of cards, sometimes by a whispered rumor.

It didn't take long to hear the name that soured the very air.

"Cleaned him out," a silver-haired peer muttered to his companion, cradling a snifter of brandy. "Young Bellamy. Poor fool. Lost his whole bloody estate to Walsh in a single night. The one he inherited from his aunt."

"Foolish to play so deep," came the indifferent reply. "Still, he did make a scene, didn't he? Accused Walsh of cheating. Loud enough for half the club to hear."

My interest sharpened to a blade's edge.

I turned away, locking Bellamy's name in my mind, and crossed to a quiet alcove near the card tables, where the steward kept a discreet ledger of the night's games. A few sovereigns changed hands under the table. The steward, suitably encouraged, showed me the entries without protest.

"Lord Walsh played most nights this past month," he murmured. "High stakes. Several gentlemen were bled dry, including young Bellamy. Walsh always walked away heavier in the purse, no matter the hand."

I narrowed my eyes. "Did no one question it?"

The steward hesitated. "Not publicly, except for Bellamy. But more than a few said the cards felt wrong—too warm, too smooth. Not one of them dared say it aloud. Not against a man like Walsh. He was too clever."

After noting the names who'd lost the most, I thanked him with another coin and moved on.

In the reading room, between two overstuffed wingback chairs and a fire that hissed with hollow cheer, another conversation snagged my attention—sharp, bitter, and full of anger barely held in check. I recognized both gentlemen, Lord Finch and Lord Danforth.

"Damn fool promised us a fortune," Finch hissed. "Silver in the American West, he said. All we had to do was sign the papers and wait for the gold to roll in."

"I put in eight thousand pounds. You?" Danforth asked.

"Seven. Nearly put in more. Never made a penny back. Clearly, we were duped."

My hands curled into fists at my sides.

So Walsh had not been content with cheating at cards. He had conned men at their most vulnerable, fed their dreams and greed with lies, and then gutted them.

He hadn't just courted ruin. He had built his fortune atop it.

And someone had finally made him pay the price.

~

I FOUND Bellamy alone in the library, nursing what remained of a bottle of brandy like a man clinging to wreckage after a shipwreck. His youth was evident in the droop of his shoulders, the lost look in his red-rimmed eyes. His cravat was crooked, his waistcoat stained and wrinkled.

"Bellamy," I said evenly.

He flinched at the sound of his name, then sagged further when he recognized me. "Your Grace," he rasped.

I sat opposite him, ignoring the inquisitive glances of a few nearby patrons. "I hear you played cards with Walsh."

He gave a broken laugh. "Played? That's a generous word."

"Word is," I said, voice low, "you made accusations."

He stared into his glass. "He cheated. I know he did. The

way he handled the cards ... It wasn't chance. It was thievery dressed up as luck. I could feel it in my gut."

"You lost everything?"

He laughed again. A bitter, hollow sound. "The manor house I inherited. The horses. The entire bloody estate. Everything but the clothes on my back. My mother's packing as we speak. Unless I find a wealthy wife, we'll be lucky to find rooms in Bloomsbury."

I studied him, weighing his grief against the raw edge of anger crackling off him.

"Loss like that breeds hatred, Bellamy," I said quietly. "And hatred, when deep enough, can drive a man to do unspeakable things."

He met my gaze, and for a moment, I saw naked, ruinous pain there.

"Are you accusing me of murder?"

"No," I said simply. "But I am asking. Where were you two nights ago?"

His face paled. He swallowed hard.

"Home," he said hoarsely. "Alone. With a bottle. No one to vouch for me." His voice broke. "But I didn't kill him. God help me, I didn't. If I had, I'd have made sure the whole bloody world knew he got what he deserved."

I believed him. Mostly. But belief was not enough. Not with so much at stake.

When I finally stepped outside, the rain had begun—a cold, misting drizzle that slicked the pavement and turned the gaslight halos into bleeding smears of gold. I pulled my collar up against the rain, my resolve hardening with every step.

Walsh had made a sport of other men's ruin. He had gambled with lives, traded dreams for dust, and reveled in the destruction he left behind. He had built a kingdom atop broken men, and now the kingdom had come crashing down around him.

The question was no longer *why* he had been murdered. That answer was painfully clear. The real question—the dangerous one—was *who* among the wreckage had finally struck the fatal blow.

As despicable as Walsh had been, he hadn't deserved to be murdered. There were other ways to bring about justice. Ruin him socially, publicly. A well-placed trap during a card game could have exposed his cheating. The silver mine scheme might have been unmasked as fraud. Either scandal would have been enough to see him banished from polite society.

But who had chosen the more final route? Could young Bellamy have done it? Or Finch or Danforth, for that matter? Perhaps even someone else entirely. An as-yet-unknown hand in this grim affair.

Someone had blood on their hands, and I wouldn't rest until I uncovered the truth.

CHAPTER
FIFTEEN

SHADOWS AT WALSH HOUSE

Before I could even pen a note to Julia asking for an audience, I received one from her. She begged my forgiveness for asking me to leave and asked if I could pay a call on her. There were matters she wished to discuss. I wasted no time making my way to Walsh House.

Upon my arrival, that residence loomed before me like a half-finished portrait—grand, certainly, but lacking warmth. Though the morning sun glinted off its stone façade and the ivy was neatly trimmed, something about the house struck a dissonant chord. As though its very walls knew that the man who had ruled it was now nothing but a name, soon to be etched on a tombstone.

The mourning draperies had already been drawn across the Walsh House doors. Heavy black crepe swathed the entrance like a shroud, an outward symbol of grief that did little to mask the turmoil coiling through the place.

I was admitted at once and shown to the morning room, where Julia awaited me.

She stood by the window when I entered, clad in mourning black, though her gown was cut simply and lacked the dramatic veils and embellishments society so often demanded of grieving widows. Her posture was ramrod straight, her fingers tightly interlaced. She turned as I approached and managed a pale smile that didn't reach her eyes.

"Rosalynd," she said, her tone apologetic. "Thank you for coming. I apologize for my behavior yesterday. I shouldn't have asked you to leave."

I gently took her hands in mine. "You were overwrought. Understandable given the circumstances."

"Thank you for understanding and attending to me in my hour of need."

"I came because I care, Julia. And also, because I'd like to ask some questions."

A flicker of something—wariness, perhaps—crossed her face. She gestured toward the settee. "Of course. Let's sit."

The silence stretched between us as the maid brought in tea and withdrew. I waited until the tea had been poured and the maid dismissed before setting my cup aside and folding my hands in my lap.

"What was it you wished to discuss, Julia?"

She hesitated, her gaze flickering toward the door, then to the fire, as though gathering the courage to speak. At last, she exhaled slowly, the tension in her posture belying the calm she tried to maintain.

"It's about Walsh," she said. "Or rather, the mess he left behind."

I said nothing, sensing she needed to unburden herself before I offered judgment or sympathy.

"The butler came to me yesterday. The staff hadn't been

paid in weeks, and the grocer has refused further deliveries. The coal merchant sent notice. No more fuel until the outstanding balance is cleared. I had to scrape together what I could from my personal allowance just to put food on the table."

I was horrified by what she'd just revealed. "Surely he hadn't neglected the accounts entirely."

She gave a small, hollow laugh. "He didn't neglect them, Rosalynd. He depleted them. Not only that, he'd been selling off valuables, piece by piece. I suspect he was gambling heavily. Again."

"Did you know?"

"I suspected," she admitted, her voice growing thinner. "But I never imagined the extent. And now there's nothing but unpaid bills and dwindling credit. I fear for what may happen to myself, the household. But most of all, I fear for my child."

"You did right to tell me," I said gently. "We'll find a way through this. Together."

Julia gave a faint nod, though the lines around her mouth remained tight with worry.

I hesitated a moment, then asked, "Was there anything else? Anything unusual you noticed in the last few weeks? Visitors, letters—anything out of place?"

She looked down at her hands, twisting the fabric of her sleeve. "There were men who came to the door. Not often, but enough for the butler to comment. Walsh never introduced them. He always met them in the study, behind closed doors."

"Did you ever overhear their conversations?"

"No. He was careful." A pause. "Too careful. But afterward, he'd be more irritable than usual. On edge."

"Did he say who they were?"

She shook her head. "Never. And if I asked, he'd fly into a rage." Her voice dropped. "Once, I found him in the library, tearing pages from a ledger and burning them in the grate."

My stomach tightened. "Do you know what was written in them?"

"I only caught a glimpse—figures, names, something scrawled in the margins. He saw me looking and slammed the book shut. Told me to stay out of his affairs if I valued what comfort I had left."

The room seemed to shrink around us.

I leaned forward slightly. "Julia, did you keep any of what you found? The receipts, the papers—anything?"

Her fingers stilled. "A few." Her eyes met mine. "I didn't know what they meant. But now..."

"You're starting to wonder what he was truly involved in."

She gave the barest nod. "And whether his death was really so simple after all."

"Did Walsh have any close acquaintances? Friends he confided in?"

She gave a short, humorless laugh. "Walsh didn't have friends, Rosalynd."

"What about enemies?" I asked gently. "Disagreements? Threats?"

She hesitated, then looked away toward the window, where the gray light of London filtered through gauzy drapes. "There were plenty. More than I cared to count. He took chances, Rosalynd. Not just at cards—but in business, in reputation, in nearly every interaction. He thought himself untouchable. And perhaps he was, until now."

I leaned forward slightly. "Did he ever receive threats? Anything written? Spoken?"

Her hands tightened in her lap. "One night—perhaps two months ago—a gentleman barged into the house. I was upstairs. I only came down because I heard shouting. He was young, enraged, and claimed that Walsh had cheated him at cards. He said—'I'll get even with you if it's the last thing I do.' I remember the exact words because Walsh just laughed and called for the footman to throw him out."

"Did you recognize him?"

"No. He never gave his name, and Walsh wouldn't speak of it afterward. Said he was no one of consequence."

"And that didn't strike you as odd?"

Julia's voice dropped. "Everything struck me as odd. He could be charming when he wanted something. But behind closed doors, he was clever. Secretive. Always maneuvering. His income from the estate barely covered our expenses, or so I thought. But as I just discovered, that wasn't true. The ball was meant to convince people we were flush with money."

"But you aren't."

She nodded slowly. "The bills for the ball haven't been paid. The florist, the musicians, even the caterer. He kept pushing off their demands for payment. Promised returns were coming. Always 'just a few days more.'"

My stomach sank. "Where did he think the money would come from?"

Julia hesitated again, her voice thickening with discomfort. "He said there was an investment—a silver mine. In the American West. He convinced several gentlemen to put money into it. But I . . . I don't think it was real."

My breath caught. "How do you know?"

"I read a letter. I wasn't supposed to, but it was left open on his desk. A man was demanding answers—he'd invested a considerable sum and had not seen a penny. Said

Walsh hadn't responded to his inquiries and threatened legal action. Walsh burned the letter in the fireplace."

"Did you ask him about it?"

"He told me it was nothing." Her voice cracked slightly. "But I think he was afraid. He never said so, but I saw it in the way he started locking his study door at night. Sleeping with a pistol in the drawer."

I pressed a hand to my chest. "Why didn't you tell anyone?"

"And say what? That my husband might have swindled half of London? That our wealth was smoke and mirrors?" She looked at me with haunted eyes. "I couldn't. I was too ashamed."

"You need to inform Dodson. So he can look elsewhere for the murderer." At the very least, it would keep suspicion from falling squarely on Julia.

"Mister Hanover made the same suggestion."

"You've seen him?"

She nodded. "Last night. He apologized for the lateness of the hour. Given the circumstances, he felt it best to see me as soon as possible. He said—" she swallowed hard "—there was no concrete proof, indeed no proof at all to tie me to Walsh's murder. Still, I can't help but worry."

She was right to do so. The rumors alone not only accused her but could lead to cold, hard facts. And Dodson was not one to ignore them. He would follow the gossip to where it might lead. But there was another avenue to explore. "Did you know about his mistress?"

Her shoulders slumped in resignation. "He visited her every Tuesday and Thursday, like clockwork. It was something we no longer discussed. I'd learned long ago that confronting him only led to cruelty."

I reached across and took her hand again. "I'm so sorry."

She looked at me, eyes shining with unshed tears, and opened her mouth to respond. But the sound of a door crashing open shattered the moment.

Voices rose in the corridor.

Julia's grip tightened on my hand as a footman attempted to announce, too late, "Mr. Charles Walsh and Mrs. Lucretia Walsh—"

"That will be Lord and Lady Walsh," Lucretia Walsh declared as she entered the room.

They'd burst into the room like a gust of cold wind. Lucretia stood with all the hauteur of a woman who believed the house was already hers. "I thought it best we come in person."

Julia stood, spine stiffening. "Why?"

Lucretia's eyes swept the room, taking in the tea tray, the elegant furnishings, and finally settling on me. "Because it's time to discuss the future. This house—"

"Is still mine," Julia interrupted sharply. "At least for now."

Lucretia's mouth thinned. "Charles is the heir. He should occupy the family residence."

"Forgive me," I said, rising to stand beside Julia. "But now is not the time to hold this discussion."

"On the contrary," Lucretia snapped. "The sooner we make arrangements, the better. There are certain expectations—"

"Expectations can wait," said another voice.

Edwin Heller had followed his cousin and his wife into the room. "Forgive the intrusion. I'd hoped to arrive before they did." He entered with an apologetic look.

Lucretia sniffed. "You always were too soft-hearted, Edwin."

He ignored her and spoke directly to Julia. "Charles doesn't expect you to leave this very moment. Not before the funeral. Not while you're still grieving. Proper arrangements can be discussed afterwards."

"Thank you," Julia whispered, voice trembling.

Charles finally spoke, his voice low. "Of course. We don't wish to rush you, Julia."

Lucretia opened her mouth again, but I cut in before she could strike. "Julia will need time. And support. Your father's will needs to be read. He had to have made arrangements for Julia. For all you know, he wished her to remain here until the birth of the babe."

Lucretia's head spun toward her husband. "He can't do that, can he, Charles? After all, he's dead."

Charles flinched. "For the love of God, Lucretia. If that is what Father desired, of course, I will honor his wishes. I would never go against them. Let us wait and see what the will says."

His attitude had undergone a drastic change since the last time I saw him. Maybe he'd had a change of heart after branding Julia a murderer. I doubted it. More than likely, his cousin had talked some sense into him. It simply would not do to call his stepmother a murderess when there was no evidence to suggest such a thing. Never mind tossing Julia from her home while she was expecting a child was bound to cause a huge scandal. His honor would be besmirched before he even assumed the title.

But that did not seem to matter to his wife, who quickly turned on him. "You're a weakling, Charles, in more ways than one. I never should have married you."

Charles shifted uncomfortably. Edwin murmured

something about needing to speak with the family solicitor and deftly ushered his cousin and Lucretia out of the room.

The moment the door closed behind them, Julia's composure crumbled. She sank onto the settee and buried her face in her hands, her shoulders shaking with silent sobs. I slipped beside her, wrapping an arm around her as she trembled beneath the weight of it all.

"I've tried so hard," she gasped. "To keep up appearances. To keep things running. And now—now it's all unraveling. The house, the lies, the debts. All of it."

"You don't have to do it alone anymore," I murmured. "You have me. And you will get through this."

She turned her face toward me, tear-streaked and pale. "You don't know how much I needed to hear that. Will you attend the inquest with me? It's scheduled for Tuesday."

"Of course, I will," I said, pressing her hand. I would need to send a note to Steele. He would want to be there.

"I'd like to search Walsh's study," I said carefully. "Perhaps there's something there that might point us toward the murderer."

Julia shook her head, her voice edged with weariness. "Inspector Dodson combed through it last night. He claimed there was nothing of interest." She paused, then added with quiet certainty, "But I wasn't surprised. My husband never kept anything important there. His ledgers and confidential papers were always locked in the hidden safe in his private quarters."

"You didn't share that with Dodson, did you?" I asked, keeping my voice low, though my pulse had begun to race.

Julia's mouth tightened. "No. I don't trust the man."

"Neither does Steele," I said, relieved. "You did the right thing by holding it back." I hesitated, then added gently, "Do I have your permission to explore Walsh's rooms?"

She nodded, though the motion was slow and burdened. "I hope you find something," she murmured. "Anything to stop this madness."

"I'll tell you if I do," I promised. "Do you know the combination to the safe?"

Her gaze lifted to meet mine, and for a moment, something fragile and aching shimmered in her eyes. "Our wedding date," she said softly. "He was hopeful then. He believed in us. But as the years passed without a child, that hope soured. He became distant. Cold. But he never changed the numbers. That's what I'll remember. That once, at least, I meant something to him."

Her voice trembled at the end, and I wanted to believe her memory was enough to tether her to peace. But the truth pressed heavily on my chest. The man she'd married may have once been kind, but the one who'd died had been cruel, controlling, and worse. I'd seen the bruises, even if she hadn't spoken of them.

If Dodson ever learned of them—if he suspected that those bruises told a motive—he would not hesitate to use them against her.

CHAPTER
SIXTEEN

ROSALYND QUESTIONS THE WALSH HOUSE STAFF

After searching Walsh's quarters and finding much more than I expected, it was time to question the staff. Of course, I would need to start with the butler. Nothing happened in that house he did not know about. Approaching him, I asked, "Would it be possible to have a few words with you, Mr. Anstruther?" I asked. "And afterward, Lord Walsh's valet?"

A flicker of hesitation crossed his face—gone almost before I could mark it.

"Of course, milady. Shall we speak in the library?"

The house seemed to absorb sound as I followed him down the corridor, the thick carpets swallowing my footsteps. Every room we passed felt emptied of life, stripped bare by fear and suspicion. Walsh's death had left more than grief behind; it had sown seeds of uncertainty that were already taking root.

Anstruther closed the library door behind us, the click of the latch unnervingly final.

He stood at attention, hands folded before him, a picture of proper dignity.

"I know these are difficult days, Mr. Anstruther," I began gently. "But anything you might recall could help resolve matters quietly."

He inclined his head. "I will assist where I can, milady."

"Tell me," I said, "did Lord Walsh have any… unpleasant encounters in the days leading up to the ball?"

A pause. Too long.

"There were visitors," he admitted finally. "Some men of business. Others, gentlemen of quality, if you take my meaning. Per Lord Walsh's orders, they were admitted to the small sitting room."

"And did Lord Walsh meet with them willingly?"

Another pause, deeper now.

"He was … reluctant," Anstruther said carefully. "But he did agree to talk to most of them. Not all, though. Some were denied entry."

"Who were these men?"

He provided me with several names. Some I recognized; others I did not. "There were raised voices on more than one occasion."

"Did you perhaps note what the discussions were about?"

"I did not hear the entire discussions. But I did catch several words."

"Of course." He was reluctant to admit he'd eavesdropped, like any good butler would. "And what were those words?"

"Thief, card sharp, swindler."

None of his visitors had a good opinion of Walsh, that was certain.

"Anything else you can think of, Mr. Anstruther?"

"Not at the moment, milady."

"If you think of anything else, could you please send word to Rosehaven House?"

"Of course, milady."

"Thank you, Mr. Anstruther. I would like to speak with Lord Walsh's valet now, if I may."

He hesitated but finally dipped his head and rang a bell.

Moments later, a thin, nervous-looking young man entered the room. His livery hung loosely on his frame, and he twisted his hands with visible anxiety.

"This is Phipps," Anstruther said shortly. "Lord Walsh's valet."

I smiled warmly. "Thank you for seeing me, Mr. Phipps. I know this must be a difficult time."

Phipps swallowed hard. "Yes, milady."

"I would only like to ask a few questions. You were close to Lord Walsh—you saw him daily. Did you notice any changes in him recently?"

Phipps shifted on his feet. "He was ... troubled, milady. Jumpier than usual. Locked his chambers more often. Kept looking over his shoulder."

"Was there anyone he argued with?"

The young man hesitated. "Not in front of me, no. But ..."

He darted a glance toward Anstruther.

"You must tell Lady Rosalynd what you know, Phipps."

"Yes, of course." Phipps turned back to me

"But?" I prompted gently.

Phipps licked his lips. "The night before the ball, someone came to the house. Late. After midnight."

"Did you see who it was?"

"No, milady. I only heard the shouting. Lord Walsh's

voice and another man's. Angry. Real angry. I heard something about payment."

My heart quickened. "Payment for what?"

"I don't know, milady. I swear it. But afterward, Lord Walsh looked like he'd seen a ghost."

"Did you know about this visitor, Mr. Anstruther?"

"No. I'm sorry to say I was suffering from a toothache. But one of the footmen would have opened the door. Once I find out who, I'll have a word with him."

As I turned back to Phipps, he appeared ready to collapse. Miserable did not begin to describe him.

I offered him a reassuring smile. "You've been most helpful. Thank you."

After dismissing Phipps, I lingered in the library alone, pretending to examine a volume of Dryden's poetry. But my mind raced as I considered the implications of everything I'd learned. Someone had confronted Walsh the night before his death over money. A large debt? A failed scheme? The pieces were beginning to shift, but the picture they formed remained maddeningly incomplete.

Maybe the study held some answers. Once I arrived there, I carefully inspected the desk. I ran my fingers along the edge of it. An elegant piece, though softened by years of use. I bent closer, inspecting its details with a practiced eye. On the underside of the top drawer, something had been scratched into the wood.

Curious, I tugged the drawer open and slipped my hand beneath the lip. My fingers brushed against something dry and crumpled. Heart pounding, I carefully drew it out.

It was a torn scrap of ledger paper. The ink had smudged, but several words remained legible—and damning:

"Transfer — E.L. Bank — to account #9431"

A hidden transaction, maybe of concealed funds. A trail Walsh had deliberately tried to erase.

I folded the fragment and slipped it into my reticule, my thoughts already racing. Steele would need to locate that bank. Trace the account. Maybe we'd find funds there.

After securing Julia's permission to take the ledgers and documents I'd retrieved from the safe, I bid her farewell. One of Rosehaven's footmen would deliver them to Steele with a note.

I was willing to wager that something in those pages had sparked the fire that led to Walsh's murder.

And I had just caught the scent.

CHAPTER
SEVENTEEN

A DOOR WITHOUT ANSWERS

The address I'd pried from a reluctant member at White's was tucked along a quiet, grim little street in the less than desirable, but still acceptable, streets of Clerkenwell—one of those aging rows of brick where the city's gloss had worn thin, and the business of men with sharp smiles and sharper deals thrived behind discreet plaques.

I had no great hopes as I approached. Men like Walsh didn't leave their real sins lying about where any curious soul might stumble across them. Still, even a spider's web left clues if you knew how to look.

A discreet brass plate beside the door read simply: "*Great Western Silver Trust.*"

I rapped once with my cane, sharp against the fog-muffled afternoon.

A young man—no more than five and twenty—opened the door. He wore a neat if threadbare jacket, a clerk's ink-stained fingers, and the wary expression of a man accustomed to saying as little as possible.

"Good afternoon, sir," he said, eyeing me with cautious civility. "May I assist you?"

"I'm here about Lord Walsh," I said smoothly. "Your employer."

The clerk paled visibly, confirming more in that instant than he realized. "I—I'm not sure what you mean, sir. I only manage the post."

"Indeed," I said, stepping over the threshold without invitation. He retreated automatically, leading me into a narrow vestibule lined with battered filing cabinets and the faint, musty smell of old paper. No other living soul was there. Nor did there appear to be any documents of recent vintage. The place was bare—bare of true business, bare of wealth. A false front. No real company worked out of these rooms.

"You handle messages?" I inquired. Clearly, that was the only purpose for his presence.

"Y-yes, sir," he stammered. "I was instructed to receive communications addressed to the Great Western Silver Trust and forward them to Lord Walsh. That's all. I swear it."

"Who sent them?"

A flicker of hesitation.

"Tell me," I said quietly.

He swallowed hard. "They were mostly from gentlemen. But some were anonymous. A few names came up more than once. Lord Danforth. Lord Finch. Mr. Halwell."

I filed the names away. All men of means. All known in society. "What about the contents?" I asked. "Any impressions?"

The clerk hesitated. "They were usually short. Urgent.

Some spoke of 'installments' or 'shares.' Others simply requested meetings. A few warned of consequences if promises weren't kept."

In other words, threats. Walsh had promised wealth and delivered ruin, and now even his own backers had begun to turn on him.

"Did you handle any payments?" I pressed.

The clerk shook his head violently. "No, sir. Only papers. If money changed hands, it wasn't here."

I believed him. The poor fool looked ready to faint at the mere suggestion.

Walsh had spearheaded a scheme meant to attract capital with the promise of greater gains. And a number of fools believed him. But he couldn't have acted alone. No one in their right mind would have taken Walsh's sole word for it. That would need investigating.

"Did you copy the messages?"

"Oh, no, sir. I wouldn't do that. It was private correspondence. I just read them, that's all, as instructed by Lord Walsh."

"Do you remember who warned of consequences?"

"Lord Finch and Lord Danforth."

"What about Mr. Halwell?"

"He wanted his money back. He was quite insistent."

I grew impatient. "What did it say?"

"No more delays, no more dodging. I want my money back—*with interest*."

I left the clerk with a warning to forget I had ever been there, though I doubted he would sleep soundly for a month.

As I stepped back into the misty London afternoon, I allowed myself a grim smile.

CHAPTER EIGHTEEN

THE WEIGHT OF TESTIMONY

The following Tuesday, the inquest was held in a hushed, oak-paneled chamber within the Coroner's Court, the air heavy with the scent of old books and older judgment. Outside, a spring drizzle dampened the pavement, but inside, the atmosphere was dry as tinder—and just as flammable. Whispers drifted like smoke through the room as Julia and I made our way down the narrow aisle.

She was dressed in mourning black from head to toe, a veil obscuring her face, though nothing could conceal the tension in her posture or the way her gloved hands clutched her reticule as though it were a lifeline.

A row at the front had been reserved for the family. Julia was guided to her place, and I took the seat beside her. On her other side sat the Walsh family solicitor, Mr. Greaves, his expression unreadable. The remainder of the bench was occupied by Charles Walsh, his harpy of a wife, Lucretia, and their cousin, Edwin Heller, who appeared appropriately somber.

A few rows back, the Duke of Steele had taken a seat. His presence was discreet—deliberately so—but no less notable for it.

The coroner, a thin man with a mouth like a straight line drawn in ink, opened proceedings with brisk efficiency. He wasted no time calling the first witness, the police constable who'd discovered Walsh's body.

"I was making my regular rounds," said the officer, a barrel-chested man in a damp uniform that still bore traces of the rain. "Passed by Hanbury Street at a quarter past midnight. Body wasn't there then. Found him just before one. So he'd been dead less than an hour."

"And the scene?" the coroner asked.

"No signs of struggle. Just Lord Walsh, slumped against the wall. Looked like he fell where he stood." He cleared his throat. "Of course, it was not natural. There was blood all over him."

No cries, no chase. Just silence and sudden death. Julia made no sound, but I saw the faintest tremor in her fingers.

The next witness entered with an air of practiced humility. Her black dress was modest, her hair pinned simply. She folded her hands and kept her eyes downcast—the perfect picture of a respectable widow. But even I could see through it. The court could, too. There was nothing respectable about Mrs. Evangeline Pratt.

"Lord Walsh was a friend of my late husband's," she said softly. "He visited from time to time. Out of kindness, you see."

Kindness. That word clanged in the room like a cracked bell.

"And the night in question?" the coroner asked.

"He came around eight. Stayed for tea. Left around half eleven."

"You shared tea?" the coroner said.

"And conversation. Nothing more."

The way she tried to dress up the truth in clean linen would have been comical if it weren't so tragic. Walsh hadn't gone to her for conversation. He'd kept her. She was his mistress, veils and tea notwithstanding.

Next came the medical examiner who wasted no time with his testimony. "Single stab wound to the heart," he intoned. "Blade entered cleanly between the ribs. Death was instantaneous."

"Would it require strength?"

"No. Only precision. The sort of placement that suggests familiarity with the anatomy."

Julia did not flinch, but the room seemed to draw tighter around her.

Then came Dodson, smug and iron-backed.

"We have reason to believe Lord Walsh was the victim of a professional killing," he said.

"On what grounds?" the coroner asked.

"The nature of the wound. The lack of struggle. The target's connections to business schemes of questionable legality."

"And do you have a suspect in mind?"

Dodson looked directly at Julia.

"Not at present. But I believe the killer was hired by someone close to him."

The implication was clear. Murmurs stirred. I felt my jaw clench.

The coroner, to his credit, cut him off. "Chief Inspector, this inquest is to determine cause of death, not speculate on motives or guilt."

"Understood," Dodson said, though his voice oozed satisfaction.

The jury filed back in less than an hour.

"We find that Lord Percival Walsh met his death by a wound inflicted with intent by person or persons unknown."

A neat phrase to wrap a bloody truth.

As we rose, Julia let out a quiet breath, the first she'd allowed herself since the proceedings began. I gently looped my arm through hers and escorted her outside where the wind tugged at her veil.

She did not speak until we were safely within the carriage.

"They all think I did it," she whispered.

I met her gaze. "Then we shall prove you didn't."

And in my heart, I silently vowed—no matter the cost.

CHAPTER
NINETEEN

THE READING OF THE WILL

The next morning, we assembled in the drawing room, a cold, sunless chamber in Walsh House that had always struck me as oppressively formal. Today, it felt more like a courtroom. The solicitor, a wiry man named Mister Greaves with spectacles perched precariously on his nose, had arranged himself behind a table stacked with paperwork, every sheet bristling with legal finality.

Julia sat beside me, cloaked in unrelenting black. A veil concealed her face, but the rigid line of her shoulders and the way her gloved hands twisted tightly in her lap spoke volumes. Across the room, Charles and Lucretia shared a small settee. Charles's expression remained unreadable, but Lucretia looked positively radiant, as though Christmas had arrived early. Edwin Heller, Charles's cousin, was also present. His position as heir presumptive gave him the right to attend, but I suspected his presence had less to do with legal entitlement and more to do with managing Charles.

Any burst of emotion, especially anger, might provoke trouble with his cousin's heart.

As the solicitor began the reading of the will, a maid glided silently into the room bearing a silver tea tray. The fine porcelain cups clinked gently as they were distributed, a soft domestic counterpoint to the solemnity of the proceedings. Charles accepted his with the air of a man reclaiming a small pleasure in difficult circumstances. He took a thoughtful sip, then gave a satisfied nod.

"This is rather excellent," he said, glancing toward Julia. "Is it Darjeeling?"

Julia's voice was quiet behind her veil, but steady. "It's a special blend," she replied. "I'll send a packet to you."

Charles inclined his head in appreciation and took another sip, entirely unaware of how neatly the moment would lodge itself in memory—harmless, courteous, and, as it seemed then, entirely unremarkable.

Mister Greaves cleared his throat with bureaucratic precision. "We are gathered here to read the last will and testament of the late Lord Percival Walsh. As his solicitor, I am bound to convey his final wishes exactly as set forth in this document."

No one spoke.

He began with the formalities—titles, holdings, clauses that only the most devoted legal mind could decipher. Julia's grip on her gloves tightened with each passing line.

"To my son, the Honourable Charles Walsh, I bequeath the Walsh estate in its entirety," Greaves read. "Including properties, furnishings, household staff, and all accompanying entitlements."

Charles gave no visible reaction. Lucretia, however, sat up straighter, her eyes gleaming.

"To Lady Lucretia Walsh, wife of the Honourable

Charles Walsh, I leave the Walsh pearls and the portrait of the first Lady Walsh currently hanging in the blue salon."

My stomach twisted. Still nothing for Julia.

"And to my wife, Lady Julia Walsh," Mister Greaves said at last, "I leave the Dower House, per the terms of the marriage contract." He looked up, blinking. "There are no additional bequests."

The silence that followed was louder than any shout.

"No additional bequests?" Julia's voice was paper-thin.

"I'm afraid not, milady," Mister Greaves said.

Julia stood so suddenly her chair scraped harshly against the floor. "Then how am I meant to live? How am I to raise our child?"

My heart clenched. I rose at once and took her arm. "You'll come with me to Rosehaven House. You'll stay with us. We'll provide for you."

Julia swayed, and I feared for a moment she might faint. "I have nothing," she whispered. "Less than nothing. I don't even have a wardrobe suitable for mourning." She glanced down. "Except for this gown."

"You have us," I said firmly. "And we will see to everything."

Behind us, Lucretia exhaled a little laugh, quickly smothered. But I saw the way she practically bounced on the settee cushion, her eyes already measuring drapery and carpeting, likely envisioning herself presiding over the Walsh drawing room with all the grace of a particularly smug cat.

"Perhaps," she said, her voice syrupy, "we might begin redecorating once the house is officially ours."

I turned, slow and deliberate. "You may begin when Lady Julia has moved out and not a moment before."

Her smile faltered.

Good.

As I guided Julia from the room, I couldn't help but think that the dead could still wound the living in ways more vicious than any dagger. Walsh had not just abandoned his wife in death. He had ensured her humiliation, her ruin.

But she would not fall. Not while I drew breath.

She was coming home with me.

CHAPTER TWENTY

A MEETING OF SECRETS

The Chelsea House butler, formal, dignified, and composed to the point of stillness, opened the door with a nod so crisp it could have sliced paper. "His Grace is expecting you, milady," he intoned.

Without a sound, he ushered me down a narrow-paneled corridor and into the front sitting room where Steele waited by the fire. Dressed, as always, in unrelenting black, he looked as if he had just stepped out of a portrait titled The Art of Intimidation. Not a thread out of place, not a button askew. Even the faint gleam of firelight across his dark hair seemed deliberate.

And here I was—windblown, flustered, and achingly aware of both.

It wasn't entirely my fault. After the reading of the will, I'd rushed home to change for the meeting with Steele, only to discover a minor disaster had erupted at Rosehaven House. The calamity involved Chrissie's new ball gown—the wrong one had been delivered. Instead of the soft green silk we'd commissioned, she'd received a ghastly confection of mauve and mustard yellow that would have made a peacock blush. Tracking down the modiste, retrieving the correct gown, and soothing Chrissie's inevitable tears had eaten up the better part of my afternoon—and my patience.

"Forgive my tardiness," I said briskly. "There was a situation at home. A wayward ball gown and a missing modiste."

His lips twitched. "Managing younger siblings sounds remarkably like herding lunatics through a haberdashery."

I stiffened. "They are not lunatics."

A glint of amusement softened into something closer to regret. "No disrespect meant, Lady Rosalynd. Only admiration for your resilience."

Some of the indignation bled from my spine, but I offered him a cool nod. I would forgive the slight—eventually.

"Would you care to sit?" he asked, gesturing toward one of the chairs.

After a brief hesitation, I obliged. The chair was as comfortable as it was elegant.

"Tea and biscuits will be served shortly," he added, settling into the armchair opposite.

"I'd prefer brandy."

His lips quirked, a flicker of amusement dancing in his eyes, no doubt recalling our last encounter when he'd forsaken Earl Grey for something stronger.

"Of course."

He tugged the bell pull, and the butler reappeared almost at once. After giving his order, Steele remained silent, allowing me a quiet moment to take in the room.

The Queen Anne furnishings were polished to a soft

glow. A walnut settee with delicately curved legs, an antique escritoire beneath a gilt-framed mirror, a pair of Chippendale chairs upholstered in rich damask.

This was no bachelor's bolt-hole.

Everything whispered wealth—not the gaudy, ostentatious sort, but a cultivated, inherited ease. Even the air smelled faintly of lavender polish and old wood.

In Chelsea, of all places.

A fire crackled in the hearth, sending flickering light across dark-paneled walls and exquisite furniture. No clutter. No signs of life. A house seemingly without a resident.

And yet, it had a butler. A cook and a maid as well. The house was spotless, and biscuits did not bake themselves.

Feeling an unexpected prick of irritation, I tucked my gloves more firmly beneath my hands.

It was obvious who resided here. His lover. When he had one, that is. Claire had said he was between mistresses. A man like Steele would need somewhere discreet, somewhere the curious eyes of Mayfair society could not follow.

I was surprised by how much that thought rankled.

"I had not thought Chelsea your preferred neighborhood," I said lightly.

A flicker of amusement passed over his face. "It suits its purpose."

"And what purpose is that?" I asked, sharper than I intended.

"Privacy," he answered simply. "Nothing more."

No mention of mistresses. No denial either.

Infuriating man.

The butler entered with a decanter and two snifters. After he left, Steele splashed generous portions into both. As he handed one to me, his gaze found mine—steady, assessing, always a touch too perceptive for comfort.

"You did take a hackney?"

My hackles bristled. "Of course, I'm not completely devoid of sense." When he said nothing, I felt ashamed. "I apologize. It's been a trying day."

"You carry a lot of responsibilities. More than likely, you'd prefer to be sitting at home, knitting."

I belted out a laugh. "Not my forte, Steele. When I have the rare few minutes to indulge myself, I read or write."

"Passionate petitions to the House of Lords?"

"Sometimes, but mostly I keep a journal."

"And what do you write in it?"

I gazed at him in surprise.

"My turn to apologize. Your thoughts are private."

"Some are. I won't share them with you. But others involve the management of the household. Supplies that must be ordered, tasks that must be performed. Once a week, I meet with our housekeeper and discuss them with her."

"Once Rosehaven marries, his wife will take over that task."

"My brother hasn't shown any movement in that direction. But he has time. He's only eight and twenty."

"I married when I was five and twenty."

"That young?"

"I was in love, Lady Rosalynd."

The words landed between us like a stone dropped in still water.

He came to his feet, restlessness written in every line of his frame. I felt it, too—something unspoken rising between us. Dangerous. Unwise.

It was safer to move to the matter at hand. "Shall we proceed with our reports?"

He inclined his head, a consent of sorts.

"As you know, I made some discoveries at Walsh House." I'd had the documents delivered to Steele by one of our footmen.

"The ledgers."

"Yes. But there was more." I told him of the debts that had piled up. I shared Julia's fears, now compounded by Charles's wife's hostility.

A flicker of sympathy cut across his face. "Your cousin is suffering unduly."

"Through no fault of her own," I added.

He neither agreed nor disagreed.

"What did you discover?" I asked.

"I made inquiries at White's. Lord Walsh was not only cheating at cards, he was luring men into a fraudulent investment. A silver mine in America. Apparently, he promised returns that never materialized. After obtaining the address of the enterprise, I visited the offices of the Great Western Silver Trust. As I expected, it was a false front. There was only one clerk there, charged with receiving messages and forwarding them to Walsh. He did read them, though, so I have a few names to investigate.

"It does beg a troubling question," he continued. "If his debts were piling up, what did he do with the money?"

"It's not in his study or his quarters. I checked thoroughly. Nor does it appear in his bank account. Julia spoke with the banker Walsh patronized. At first, he was hesitant to disclose anything, as the will hadn't been read. But when she explained there were household bills in urgent need of payment, he relented."

I met Steele's gaze. "Walsh was nearly penniless."

His brow furrowed.

"However, I did find something in his study—wedged

beneath the lip of a drawer." I withdrew the torn scrap of ledger paper and handed it to him.

He read aloud, voice low and steady: "'Transfer — E.L. Bank — to account #9431.'"

"Do you have any idea what that refers to?" I asked.

"No," he replied, folding the scrap with care. "But I can find out."

"I hoped you could."

Steele stared at the paper a moment longer. "He must have created a secret account no one would know about." He glanced at me, the lines around his mouth tightening. "The question now becomes—why? Why hoard wealth he couldn't publicly enjoy?"

I pressed my hands together to keep them still. "Perhaps he intended to disappear," I suggested. "To flee before the noose tightened."

"Or perhaps," Steele said grimly, "he was planning something worse."

The fire crackled between us, casting dancing shadows across the room. I caught myself studying him—the hard set of his jaw, the tension in his broad shoulders.

He was not merely investigating. He was hunting. And heaven help whoever he caught.

After a moment, Steele's voice softened, though it lost none of its intensity. "We must find out where that money is before Dodson does. If he uncovers anything before we do, Lady Walsh—and my brother—may suffer for it."

I nodded once, fiercely. "Agreed."

We remained in silence, the weight of our shared task settling between us like a tangible thing. The intimacy of purpose drew us closer, yet at the same time, another possibility loomed: to save Julia, we might have to condemn Nicholas.

At length, he moved to stand before the hearth, his figure cutting a tall, commanding silhouette against the firelight.

"I'll investigate the men who invested in the silver mine. I'll visit them. Discreetly. And locate that bank."

"And I'll attend a few ladies' gatherings—teas and such. Lady Finch and Lady Danforth are bound to attend at least one. I can feel them out about their husbands' minds on an investment that went so wrong."

Steele inclined his head once, formally. "Yes, do that."

I stood and smoothed my skirts. It was time to bring our discussion to an end. "Until next time."

The butler appeared when summoned. Before I could say another word, I found myself once again in the cool, damp air of Chelsea, the door closed behind me.

I paused on the steps, drawing a slow breath, trying to shake the lingering weight of the conversation.

But as I turned toward the waiting hackney, one truth settled in my mind with stubborn, uneasy clarity.

I needed to discover the truth, even if it meant Lord Nicholas was implicated.

CHAPTER
TWENTY-ONE

THE PRICE OF SCANDAL

I spent the following day at Walsh House, assisting Julia as she sorted through her belongings and fending off a steady procession of well-wishers. They came under the guise of offering condolences, but it was clear many were more interested in sniffing out gossip about Walsh's murder. As if that weren't irritating enough, Lucretia had the sheer audacity to send a draper to measure for new curtains. Apparently, the drawing room décor didn't suit her taste. Needless to say, he was not admitted. Lucretia could measure to her heart's content *after* she'd taken up residence.

Naturally, this prompted a visit from Lucretia herself—one I could not prevent, as she was now, regrettably, the mistress of the house. I refused, however, to let her see Julia. She was already heartbroken at the thought of leaving her home. Subjecting her to polite conversation with that venom-tongued harpy would only have deepened the wound.

I received Lucretia in the drawing room, where I struggled to hold my tongue as she prattled on about her grand plans to redecorate Walsh House. Fortunately, after half an hour, the butler appeared with word that Julia required me. Lucretia finally took her leave, though not before vowing to return at first light to conduct a full inventory—just to ensure Julia hadn't taken anything that didn't belong to her. It was all I could do not to wrap my hands around that long, lily-white neck of hers.

Once every trunk had been packed and arrangements made to have Julia's belongings delivered to Rosehaven House the following morning, I made my escape. The day had worn me to the bone. My gloves were damp, my skirts clung to my legs from the damp chill, and my limbs ached from too many stairs and too few moments of rest. But worse than the physical toll was the emotional weight—the quiet, heartbreaking grief etched on Julia's face as she took one last look around what had been her home. That image stayed with me all the way back to Grosvenor Square.

By the time I reached home, I was breathless and half-frozen, the wind having clawed its way through my coat during the rattling hackney ride across town. I had barely set foot on the top step when Honeycutt opened the door, his expression unreadable save for a faint lift of his brows. I had left word I'd be returning by four. It was now close to six. I felt every minute of the delay in my bones.

After stepping aside to allow me entrance, he added with impeccable timing, "Her Ladyship, the Dowager Countess of Rosehaven, awaits you in the morning room, milady." His tone, though carefully neutral, left no doubt—this was not a social call.

A fresh wave of exhaustion swept over me. Of course,

she was here. I should have known better than to think I could end the day without one final reckoning.

I hurried upstairs, barely pausing to let Tilly strip off my cloak, boots, and gown before darting into the bathing chamber. It wouldn't do to present myself to Grandmother in all my dirt.

A quick plunge, a hasty scrubbing, and within half an hour I was buttoned into a fresh gown of sober navy wool, my hair still slightly damp at the temples. Not exactly my finest presentation. But considering the day I'd had, Grandmother should be grateful I managed a corset at all.

The morning room was warm with the scent of woodsmoke and lemon cakes when I entered. Thankfully, Grandmother was alone, which, given the look in her eye, came as no surprise. She sat in her customary chair, her cane laid across her knees like a scepter, those shrewd eyes fastened on the doorway even as I crossed it.

"Rosalynd," she said sharply. "It is half past six. You've kept me waiting."

How was I supposed to know she was coming? Still, one did not bring that up with her. "My apologies, Grandmother," I said, curtsying. "I was unexpectedly detained at Walsh House. Julia needed assistance finalizing her packing before the move."

Grandmother's eyes narrowed, but not with disapproval. "I suppose someone had to see to the poor girl," she said, her voice clipped but not unkind. "Though heaven knows, you take on far more than is wise."

I folded my hands in front of me. "She has no one, Grandmother, and she's expecting a child. She needs all the help I can give her." I drew a steadying breath, forcing my voice to remain composed. "May I ask what brings you to Grosvenor Square this evening?" Under other circumstances, I would have chosen my words more carefully. But exhaustion had worn away my usual restraint.

For a moment, she said nothing, her gaze sharp and unreadable. Then, with a flick of her wrist and a sniff that could have cut glass, she replied, "Scandal. That's what has brought me here today."

I froze. "Scandal? What scandal?"

She tapped the tip of her cane once, smartly, against the floor. "The entire of Mayfair is buzzing. Rumors, child. Rumors involving your name *and* the Duke of Steele's."

I made it to the tea table and busied myself with the cups, if only to hide the flush rising to my cheeks.

"Surely," I said lightly, "Mayfair finds someone to gossip about every week."

"This is no ordinary gossip," Grandmother snapped. "It's persistent. Repeated. Vicious. You're on the verge of courting a scandal of prodigious proportions." She leveled me with a look so withering it could have silenced Parliament. "If this continues, the only respectable course left will be for you to marry Steele."

The very idea prompted a sharp, involuntary bark of laughter. "Really, Grandmother."

"Yes, really. Now," she said, "you will tell me precisely what you are doing skulking about with the duke, or so help me, Rosalynd, I shall imagine far worse than the truth."

I sighed. There was no evading her.

Placing the cups in front of us both, I sat carefully on the edge of the settee and said, "We are investigating Lord Walsh's murder."

Grandmother blinked. "Whyever so?"

"His Grace and I believe there are certain ... issues the

authorities may overlook. Julia's future, and that of another innocent party, hangs in the balance."

"And you," Grandmother said icily, "believe it your duty to play detective?"

"In this case," I said calmly, "yes."

Grandmother set her cup down with a force that rattled the saucer.

"How does Steele fit into all this?"

At least that was one thing she hadn't discovered. "He's helping me."

"Out of the goodness of his heart?"

"He thinks it an interesting puzzle."

"Umm, more likely his brother is involved. I've heard rumors about Lord Nicholas and Julia. Are they true?"

"What rumors?"

"Don't play coy with me, Miss! It doesn't suit you and belittles me."

When I failed to comment, she said, "Do you not understand what you are risking? *Your name? Your reputation?*"

"I understand," I said, the knot in my stomach tightening.

"No, you do not," she said, voice low and cutting. "Already, the gossips murmur that you and the duke are ... entangled. They say you're meeting in Chelsea, in a secret house where illicit affairs have been known to be conducted. That you linger in his company far beyond what propriety allows."

I bit my lip.

Grandmother leaned closer, her lined face fierce with concern.

"And your sister, Rosalynd. Have you thought of Chrysanthemum? If you embroil yourself in scandal, what decent gentleman will offer for her? No man of sense will risk tying himself to a family sinking into disgrace."

The words landed like blows.

Chrissie, bright and hopeful, just beginning her season. What suitor would risk his own reputation if whispers clung to the Rosehaven name?

My chest tightened painfully.

"I am doing this for Julia," I said, my voice thickening despite myself. "She has no one else. The reading of the will was held yesterday. Walsh left her nothing but the Walsh dower house, not even the funds to manage it."

"Disgraceful." Grandmother's expression softened—slightly—but her voice remained firm. "Then you must tread carefully, child. Already, the ground crumbles beneath your feet. One misstep, and you may bring down far more than yourself."

I stirred my tea mechanically, the fire crackling too loudly in the heavy silence between us.

For the first time since I had begun this mad endeavor, doubt crept in at the edges of my resolve. Had I misjudged the cost? But then I thought of Julia's pale face, her shaking hands, the weight of injustice pressing down on her. And I knew.

I could not turn back. Not now. Not ever. Better to risk scandal—and even heartbreak—than live with cowardice on my conscience.

After Grandmama left—her cane tapping a thunderous rhythm down the hallway—I allowed myself one long, steadying breath.

The room seemed oddly hollow without her fierce presence. The fire hissed in the grate, and the air felt heavier, burdened by the warnings she had left behind. For a moment, I stood there, letting the silence settle like dust around me. But retreat was a luxury I could ill afford.

With a sigh, I made my way to my desk. There were tasks to attend to, however distasteful. Chief among them: a note to Claire. I took up my pen with no small measure of reluctance—not because I feared Claire would refuse. On the contrary, she'd be thrilled by my sudden interest in society teas. Rather, it was the prospect of immersing myself in the clucking company of gossip-hungry matrons that made my skin crawl. Women who pried, dissected, and whispered until lives lay bare like butterflies pinned beneath glass.

But desperate times, as they say.

Claire replied within the hour. Her note, penned in an exuberant hand, read:

"Dearest Rosalynd,

How positively thrilling! Lady Farnsworth is hosting tea tomorrow, and you shall be my honored guest. Prepare to be scandalized. And do bring your sharpest smile. The ladies are positively foaming over Walsh's demise. Wear something disarming."

Disarming? I thought not. I would wear my dove-gray gown with lace cuffs—elegant, modest, and entirely unmemorable. The better to fade into the background while collecting intelligence. Or so I hoped.

CHAPTER
TWENTY-TWO

TEA, TATTLE, AND TACTICS

I spent the following morning helping Julia settle into Rosehaven House. Hoping to lighten her mood, I'd chosen the brightest guest room for her. Once Julia's things were properly tucked away, her maid suggested bed rest for her. Not unexpected. It was what the doctor had recommended, after all.

There would be no bed rest for me, however—nor, indeed, any rest at all. Not that I required it. With several siblings needing attention in one form or another, I had matters to see to before dressing for Lady Farnsworth's tea.

Lady Claire had arranged to collect me at two, and though punctuality was rarely her strong suit, she arrived precisely on time—a small mercy I genuinely appreciated. Her sunny disposition, as always, lifted my spirits. The drive to Lady Farnsworth's Mayfair townhouse was brief, owing to its convenient location.

We stepped from the carriage into the bright chill of Mayfair, my gloves smooth and snug as I adjusted them with the nervous precision of someone preparing for battle rather than tea. The townhouse loomed ahead—white-bricked and respectable, with nothing at all to hint at the social carnage that often unfolded within.

I glanced at Claire, whose eyes sparkled like someone arriving at a costume ball where half the guests might be unmasked before the scones were served.

"Ready to sip scandal from china cups?" I asked under my breath.

She gave a silvery laugh. "Darling, if scandal were served on toast points, this crowd would be positively stuffed."

The front door opened before we reached it, and a footman ushered us inside with stiff decorum. Lady Farnsworth always did love a dramatic entrance, even if it wasn't her own. The drawing room was a riot of pale pastels, gilded frames, and lace doilies. The scent of jasmine tea and lemon curd wafted through the air.

"Lady Rosalynd," Lady Farnsworth cooed, squeezing my hands. "How lovely to have you among us. So rare, a lady of principle joining us vultures."

"I'm merely here for the tea," I replied.

She turned to Claire to greet her. "And Lady Edmunds, how delightful. Do come in."

The room stilled. Not silent, exactly, but the sort of pause one hears in a theatre just before the curtain lifts. I could feel the weight of their eyes—their curiosity cloaked in politeness. Then, like clockwork, conversation resumed with a touch more animation than before. As if nothing had happened. As if they hadn't all just catalogued my every move and wondered how close I truly was to the dead man's widow. And more importantly, what gossip they could pry from me.

Claire leaned in, whispering with amusement, "I do believe you've just stolen the room."

"I'd rather steal the truth," I murmured. Together we swept toward a table already occupied by Lady Ponsonby and Lady Ashcombe, who were not so much known for conversation as for strategic dissemination of information.

The tea was hot, the cakes dainty, and the conversation meandered through the usual topics—seasonal events, minor scandals, and the latest flutter of fashion. But beneath it all was something sharper. Tension. Unspoken curiosity. I might as well have walked in trailing a cloud of sulfur.

"Have you tried the violet macarons?" Lady Ponsonby asked, offering a tray with the exaggerated grace of a peace treaty.

"Thank you," Claire said smoothly while placing two on a plate. Seated beside me with her teacup poised just so, she waited until a convenient lull before speaking. "I recently came into a modest bequest," she said lightly, as if the matter were hardly worth mentioning. "Not a fortune, of course, but enough to require thoughtful consideration."

Several heads turned with interest, though no one interrupted.

"I've been wondering," she continued, glancing around the room with a pleasant smile, "if any of you have heard whispers about promising ventures. Something quiet. Respectable. Discreet." Her delivery was effortless, perfectly timed, and I offered the faintest tilt of my head in silent approval. We had rehearsed this in the carriage. Claire would cast the line, and, if anyone knew of such ventures, the bait would surely draw them out.

She leaned in slightly, her tone casual but carefully pitched. "I heard someone mention a silver mine the other day. An American one, I believe. Out West. Supposed to yield quite a return."

That drew an immediate reaction from Lady Danforth, seated nearby. Her fan paused mid-wave, and after a quick glance around the room, she leaned closer and dropped her voice to a whisper.

"My dear, do not touch anything connected to that," she said, eyes narrowing with the memory. "My husband was taken in by such a scheme not eight months ago—Nevada, I believe. Or possibly Colorado. The company claimed they'd struck a rich vein and offered shares to a very select few. All looked aboveboard. He lost eight thousand pounds before we realized it was nothing but smoke and mirrors."

Claire blinked, just enough to suggest surprise. "How dreadful."

"Utterly humiliating," Lady Danforth muttered, fanning herself once more. "And quite impossible to recover as the person who talked him into it is quite dead."

"You don't mean … ?" Claire wondered, all wide-eyed.

"Walsh."

"The gall of the man," Lady Pickering declared, gesturing with a spoonful of lemon curd. "To sell shares in a mine that doesn't even exist! My cousin lost three thousand pounds. She had to part with her diamonds."

"Diamonds! My dear, Lady Wilmot had to let go of her footman. And she was particularly fond of him."

"He promised everyone they'd be independently wealthy," Lady Farnsworth added, lowering her voice as if sharing the secrets of the Crown.

Offering a carefully arranged expression of concern, I leaned toward Claire and whispered, "We need more names."

"Was any other lady involved?" Claire asked.

"Mrs. Greystone," remarked a marchioness I barely recognized. Clearly, I hadn't spoken as discreetly as I'd thought. "She was seen leaving Walsh House close to midnight—just a few days before his death. There was no earthly reason for her to have visited Lady Walsh, as she was not acquainted with her. And most especially that late at night. She could have invested in this silver mine."

Mrs. Greystone was wealthy, discreet, and universally regarded as beyond reproach—which, in society, almost always meant she had something to hide.

There was a beat of silence, the kind that settles when something uncomfortable has been said aloud. Then Lady Farnsworth, ever the one to steer conversation in a direction she found more manageable—or perhaps more delicious—turned to me with a sympathetic tilt of her head.

"And how is Lady Walsh faring these days?" she asked, her voice honeyed with just enough pity to sting. "Such a difficult time for her, I'm sure."

I placed my teacup down with care. "She is managing as well as can be expected, thank you."

"She's staying with you at Rosehaven House, isn't she?" asked another lady. I couldn't recall her name, only that she had a chin like a small anvil and the self-righteousness to match. "How admirable of you to take her in."

There was no mistaking the tone, nor the glint in her eye. And then, as if she couldn't help herself, she added sweetly, "Though I do wonder how long Lord Nicholas will remain such a devoted visitor. These things tend to become ... complicated."

She paused just long enough to sip her tea and let the silence stretch, then added, as if idly, "And of course, it must be ever so convenient for him now that Lady Walsh is under your roof. Far fewer proprieties to navigate when one doesn't have to knock at her own front door."

The room went very still. Fans fluttered. Cups were quietly set down. I felt Claire shift slightly beside me.

I smiled, calm and cold. "Lord Nicholas is a family friend, nothing more."

"If you say so, dear," she replied with a smile as thin as lace. I could tell she didn't believe a word of it.

Lady Farnsworth gave a delicate shiver and fluttered her fan. "Walsh was never particularly charming, was he? Always prowling about like he knew something you didn't. But really—cards at church, as they say."

Claire raised a brow, her voice deceptively casual. "Are you saying he cheated?"

"Oh, brazenly," Lady Farnsworth replied. "At Lord Bickerstaff's, last winter. My cousin was livid. Of course, she couldn't prove a thing. Walsh had a gift for making the honest appear hysterical."

The conversation drifted after that, turning toward corset styles and the scandalous behavior of someone's niece who had allegedly danced with an actor onstage. But I had heard enough. The useful part of the afternoon was over.

I leaned slightly toward Claire, lifting my napkin as if to dab at my lips, and murmured behind it, "Do be a dear and fake an indisposition."

Claire gave the faintest flicker of a smile—barely more than a tightening at the corners of her mouth—then pressed a hand to her temple.

"Oh," she said softly, with a flutter of her lashes. "I do believe I'm getting one of my dreadful headaches. Such a pity, I was enjoying myself."

Several ladies offered murmurs of sympathy, and Lady Farnsworth immediately rang for a footman.

"Such a delicate constitution," someone murmured.

"Maybe that's why she never gave Edmunds a child," said another vicious-tongued harpy.

Ignoring the jibe, I rose, all concern. "I'd best take her home at once. Poor thing can barely stand bright light when she gets one of her megrims."

With Claire leaning ever so slightly on my arm, we made our polite farewells and were ushered out with the usual pleasantries trailing behind us.

Once inside the carriage, Claire said, "That," she said, brushing an imaginary crumb from her sleeve, "was altogether too easy."

"I thought it rather distasteful." Gossip might be mother's milk to her, but I loathed it. Too many lives were shattered by remarks dropped with casual cruelty over cups of tea.

"But you got what you came for?" she inquired.

"Gossip laced with truth," I said. "The challenge now will be separating the wheat from the chaff." I would need to unravel the tangled threads we'd gathered—some truth, some fabrication, and far too much veiled behind genteel smiles. Untangling one from the other would be no simple task. But one thing was certain. I would need to meet with Steele again. We had decisions to make and precious little time to make them.

"You were brilliant," she said breezily. "You only looked horrified twice."

"Three times," I muttered. "Possibly four." I reached across to squeeze her hand. "But I am grateful for your assistance. Thank you, Claire. I owe you."

"You owe me nothing," she said with a wave of her fingers. "But I expect a full accounting when it's all solved."

I managed a smile, but unease had already begun to coil tightly in my chest. The web we were entangled in was more vast than I'd imagined. How in heaven's name were we meant to unravel it all?

But the day held one final blow. Upon returning to Rosehaven House, I was met with alarming news—Petunia was missing.

CHAPTER
TWENTY-THREE

A VISITOR OF THE MOST UNUSUAL SORT

I was drowning in paperwork—and had no one to blame but myself. Immersed as I'd been in the work of the House of Lords and the investigation into Walsh's murder, I'd let my responsibilities pile up like snowdrifts in January. My secretary, never one to mince words, warned me that if I didn't attend to them soon, the estate would begin unraveling at the seams. So I dutifully, regrettably, miserably turned to the stack.

Land disputes, tenant grievances, crop rotations, drainage reports, and one interminable argument about mortar—specifically, whether the dam on the northern boundary would hold better with lime or Portland. It was enough to make a man yearn for pistols at dawn.

So when a firm knock interrupted my bureaucratic misery, I dropped my pen with something dangerously close to gratitude.

Milford entered a moment later, as crisp and composed

as ever. "Begging your pardon, Your Grace," he said with impeccable gravity, "but Lady Petunia has come to call."

I blinked. "Lady—?"

But it was too late. She was already through the door.

Petunia Rosehaven, aged seven, stood proudly on the threshold like a miniature general who'd just seized a fortress. Her ribbon hung at a perilous angle, her cheeks were flushed with triumph, and her hands were clasped behind her back in a posture of self-satisfaction I knew entirely too well from her elder sister. "I've come for tea, Your Grace," she announced. "I trust biscuits will be served shortly? I would like fairy cakes, if possible."

I blinked again. "Fairy cakes." She'd mentioned them before.

"Preferably with icing. But not the bright pink kind. That tastes like soap."

Milford bowed, his expression the very picture of butlerly composure—though the slight twitch at the corner of his mouth betrayed his valiant struggle not to smile.

I set down my pen with a sigh, somewhere between resignation and reluctant amusement. "We can't possibly disappoint our guest, Milford," I said. "See if Cook can manage tea and fairy cakes. Lavender icing, if possible. But absolutely no pink. Evidently, it tastes like soap."

Milford, ever the professional, gave a dignified nod. "I shall convey Lady Petunia's preferences with the appropriate gravity, Your Grace."

He withdrew with the smooth efficiency of a man long practiced in navigating absurdity—though I'd wager he was smiling before he reached the corridor.

"Are you here on behalf of Lady Rosalynd?" I much doubted it, but it was the only reason that occurred to me.

Lady Petunia swung her legs over the edge of the

nearest chair. "I'm here on behalf of myself. I wanted to inspect the bedchambers."

I blinked. "The bedchambers?"

She nodded solemnly. "I need to choose one for when I move in."

"When you *what*?"

"Move in," she repeated patiently. "Grandmother says you and Rosie are courting a scandal of prodigious proportions. Something about being seen in a place called Chelsea. Which sounds frightfully dull, if I'm being honest."

"Were we, by Jove?" I muttered. How did that happen? No one of quality ever visited Chelsea.

"When people court scandal, they must marry or else everyone becomes very cross. And once you're married, I shall be moving in with you. I prefer a bed with a canopy, if you please."

I stared at her. "You're very ... efficient."

"Laurel says I'm a menace. If I'm a menace, what does that make Holly and Ivy?"

The twins who had a light of mischief in their eyes, if I recalled correctly. Lady Petunia seemed to have a point.

Milford returned some minutes later, hands neatly folded behind his back, his expression polished but contrite. "My apologies, Your Grace. The fairy cakes were not immediately available. However, Mrs. Weatherby has taken the matter in hand and assures me they are baking as we speak."

Lady Petunia gave a solemn nod. "She is to be commended."

Milford bowed slightly—whether to me or to her, I wasn't certain—and departed with the quiet efficiency of a man who'd realized that fairy cakes might one day take precedence over dukes.

Petunia turned to me with that fearless sparkle all Rosehavens seemed born with. "Since we've time to spare, perhaps you might show me the house?" she said, folding her hands primly. "I'd like to see the upstairs and choose my room."

I blinked. "Choose your—?"

"For when I move in," she said patiently, as though reminding a slow-witted footman. Her tone was all gentle correction, but the implication was clear: heaven help me.

Refusing to be bested by an seven-year-old, I found myself pushing to my feet. "As you wish, Lady Petunia." And with that, I led her from the study and toward the main staircase.

The second floor was quiet—unsurprisingly, as I was the only one who ever used it. I showed her into a series of guest chambers, all well-appointed in the fashion of quiet Mayfair elegance—high ceilings, carved moldings, pale wallpaper, a touch of faded grandeur.

She inspected them with a critical eye far too advanced for someone of her tender years.

"This one," she declared in front of an eastern-facing room. "I like the light. It will suit my dolls."

I had no idea what made a room suitable for a battalion of porcelain figures, but I nodded gravely. "Very well."

"And where would Rosie sleep?" she asked, glancing up at me with a spark of something perilously close to cunning.

"In the duchess's chambers," I answered before thinking better of it.

"May I see them?"

There was little point in refusing. Petunia was a force to

be reckoned with. Without a word, I led her down the corridor to the suite I hadn't entered in years and opened the door.

It lay just as it had been—walls draped in pink damask, ivory moulding soft with dust, and fragile furnishings untouched since ... well, since. Sunlight filtered in through lace curtains, and the faintest trace of lavender lingered in the air, like a memory unwilling to leave.

Petunia's nose wrinkled. "Oh no. This will have to be redecorated. Rosie abhors pink. She prefers soothing colors —blues and greens. But soft ones. Nothing garish."

"Noted."

"Was this your wife's room?" she asked, turning toward me with a gentleness that startled.

"Yes," I said, simply.

She didn't pry. For that, I was grateful.

After our brief tour, we returned to the study just as the tea service arrived—Milford wheeling it in with a grace that suggested he'd anticipated our timing precisely. A silver tray bore a steaming pot of Earl Grey, delicate china, and a plate of what must have been fairy cakes, their pale lavender icing glistening like sugar-kissed frost.

Petunia beamed. "Perfectly splendid."

And for the moment—however improbable it seemed —I almost agreed with her.

Now resigned to the logic of seven-year-olds, I poured tea into her cup and tried not to ponder the implications of being so thoroughly domesticated by someone under four feet tall.

"So tell me, Lady Petunia," I said with mock solemnity, "will anyone notice you've vanished?"

"Oh, eventually. At teatime, certainly. But we have at least a half hour." With the poise of a seasoned duchess, she nibbled delicately at a fairy cake. "Your cook is a treasure. You ought to increase her wages."

I chuckled, surprised by the warmth the sound brought to my own ears. "I shall give it serious consideration."

She looked at me over the rim of her teacup, eyes far too knowing for someone of seven. "You like me now. But you didn't when we first met. Why was that?"

It caught me off guard—how easily she saw through things. Rosalynd had warned me she was sharp, but I hadn't expected to be disarmed so thoroughly by someone whose feet didn't yet reach the floor.

"Well?" she prompted gently, not unkindly.

I took a breath, steadying myself. "You reminded me of my daughter."

Her eyes widened. "But you said you didn't have children."

"I don't." My voice was quieter now. "She passed away."

Petunia's face softened with something far older than her years. "Was she like me?"

"She lived but a few minutes," I said, the words catching despite how long they'd been buried. "Complications at birth."

A pause, then a whisper of sorrow in her voice. "I'm so sorry."

"So am I," I admitted. "I miss her every day. More than I can say."

She reached across the tea table and placed a small hand over mine. It was a child's gesture—simple, direct, and devastatingly kind.

"I think she would have liked fairy cakes," she said.

I couldn't speak for a moment. I could only nod.

The poignant moment shattered as the door burst open and an out-of-breath Rosalynd, her hat askew, fury radiating from her eyes, stormed into the room. "Petunia Marigold Rosehaven! Have you *lost* your mind?"

Petunia, completely unfazed, dabbed her lips with a linen napkin. "The duke and I were just having tea."

Milford quietly closed the door behind Lady Rosalynd —a wise move, as the skirmish ahead promised to escalate into something truly formidable.

I stood, bowing slightly. "Lady Rosalynd, I was honored by your sister's unexpected visit."

"I *do apologize*, Your Grace," Rosalynd said, mortified. "She escaped her maid. We searched Rosehaven House top to bottom, and then Grosvenor Square. That's where we discovered she'd come here." Glaring at her sister, she snapped out, "No fairy cakes for you."

Petunia smiled beatifically as she reached for another fairy cake, unbothered. "The duke's cook made some just for me. She's perfectly splendid. You should keep her once you marry the duke."

"When I do what?" Lady Rosalynd's voice rose to a pitch that might have startled nearby sparrows.

Petunia gave her the same look she'd given me—mild disbelief that someone could be so slow.

"When you and the duke marry," she said, entirely matter-of-factly.

"I am not. Marrying. The duke." Each word clipped and carefully enunciated, as though restraining herself from throttling the child on the spot. "Where on earth did you get that idea?"

"Grandmother. She said you're courting scandal in a house used for illicit affairs." Her brow wrinkled as she gazed at Rosalynd. "What does illicit mean?"

Rosalynd's face flushed bright red. "Never mind, you horrid child." She grabbed Petunia's hand and yanked open the door. Seemingly half of my staff was standing right outside, including Milford, who was having a hard time keeping a straight face. They dispersed immediately.

As Rosalynd escorted her sister out of the room and down the corridor, Petunia offered one last parting shot.

"Next time, I shall expect raspberry jam."

CHAPTER
TWENTY-FOUR

THE DUCHESS COMES TO CALL

The following morning, I found myself enjoying a rare moment of peace in the morning room. The children were absorbed in their lessons, Julia had taken to the garden for a morning stroll, and Chrissie was at the pianoforte—her playing as skillful as it was spirited. She didn't simply excel at the instrument; she adored it. Though I suppose the two often went hand in hand. The soft strains of one of her favorite pieces drifted through the house, lending a gentle rhythm to the morning. I allowed myself a breath—a real one, full and unguarded—grateful that, at least for now, all seemed right in my little corner of the world.

I was just finishing a note to Steele, offering yet another apology for Petunia's unscheduled visit and requesting a meeting to discuss my latest findings, when Mr. Honeycutt appeared in the doorway—his usual composure conspicuously absent.

"The Duchess of Steele, milady," he announced, somewhat flustered.

For one ridiculous moment, I thought he meant the duke.

But no—the figure who swept into the room was no man. Slim and impeccably turned out, the Duchess of Steele carried herself with quiet authority and an almost palpable energy. I had seen her from a distance before—at the opera, a garden party or two—but never this close. Her silver hair gleamed beneath her hat, and her ice-blue eyes —clear and lively—missed nothing. Though age had touched her, it hadn't dulled her in the slightest. This was the woman who had raised the Duke of Steele.

Curiosity stirring, I rose and curtsied. "Your Grace."

Entirely self-possessed, she studied me with a gaze that revealed nothing and suggested everything. "Lady Rosalynd," she said, her voice warm. "I hope you'll forgive the unannounced call. I wonder if I might have a moment of your time."

"Of course, Your Grace. Please, won't you sit?" I replied, gesturing toward one of the settees. "May I offer you some tea?"

A faint smile touched her lips as she settled on the seat. "That would be most welcomed, thank you."

I turned to Mr. Honeycutt. "Tea, if you please. And something light to go with it."

He bowed and withdrew with quiet efficiency, leaving the duchess and me alone but for the distant hum of the pianoforte still drifting in from down the hall.

After I sat across from her in the matching settee, we exchanged the expected pleasantries—weather, garden roses, and the season's relentless calendar of social obligations. Her manner was poised, every word measured and appropriate, yet I sensed there was more beneath the surface—something deliberate in her restraint.

The tea arrived on a silver tray carried by a footman, followed by a maid with a plate of lemon biscuits and neatly trimmed sandwiches. Once the door clicked shut behind them, I poured for us both and handed Her Grace a fresh cup of Earl Grey.

After taking a slow sip, the duchess met my gaze directly. "Lady Rosalynd," she said, her voice still courteous but now carrying a quiet gravity, "I've come to ask something of you. A favor, if you will."

I blinked, caught off guard. "A favor, Your Grace?"

She inclined her head ever so slightly. "I am given to understand that you and my son have been ... meeting rather often, more so than propriety strictly permits."

There was no accusation in her tone, only a calm, clear-eyed concern that felt far more disarming than scorn would have been.

Still, I drew myself up with what dignity I could muster. "Your Grace," I said carefully, "with respect—if you have questions regarding the duke's activities, you should direct them to him."

Her brows lifted slightly, a hint of amusement touching her expression. "Yes, that would be the far better path, wouldn't it? Unfortunately, Warwick rarely takes it. He fears upsetting me. He's a loving son, you see. Perhaps too much so at times."

Where was she going with this?

"May I be frank with you, Lady Rosalynd?"

"Yes, of course." Curiosity had ever been my besetting sin. And in that moment, I was positively desperate to know what she truly wanted.

"Your cousin, Lady Walsh, is now residing with you."

"Yes."

"Such a tragedy," she murmured, with a subtle shake of her head. "How is she faring these days?"

I stiffened. Surely she hadn't come all this way to indulge in gossip. If so, my opinion of her would plummet at once. "As well as can be expected."

"I understand she's expecting a child."

I said nothing. Whatever curiosity she had, I had no intention of discussing Julia's private affairs.

"My son Nicholas is rumored to be the father."

"Your Grace!" I gasped, more out of shock than offense.

She waved a hand lightly, her tone matter-of-fact. "Oh, child, I don't believe that for a moment. I know Nicholas. He may be impulsive, but he would never commit such a transgression. Still, his name has been linked to hers. And we both know how stubborn rumors can be—how quickly they grow, how vicious they become, unless stopped."

"A difficult thing to accomplish," I said, carefully.

"Indeed." She set her cup down with precision. "Which brings me to the heart of the matter. I suspect that you and Warwick have involved yourselves in the investigation of Lord Walsh's death—*you*, to clear your cousin's name, and *he*, to protect my son's. Am I correct?"

She was as perceptive as she was elegant. But before I could respond, a sharp knock came at the door. Without waiting for an invitation, the duke himself strode into the room.

He paused just inside, his gaze sweeping over the scene: his mother seated with regal composure on one of the settees, me opposite her with a teacup in hand and no doubt an expression that betrayed my surprise.

"Mother," he said, bowing slightly. "Lady Rosalynd."

"Warwick," the Duchess returned in a crisp tone.

"Your Grace," I greeted him in the same manner.

He crossed the room with measured steps, stopping beside her chair. In a measured whisper, he asked, "May I ask what you're doing here?"

"Why, enjoying a perfectly pleasant cup of tea with Lady Rosalynd."

"Is that so?" Straightening, he turned his attention to me.

"Absolutely," I said, managing a smile. "Would you like a cup yourself? Earl Grey—or something stronger?"

"No. Thank you."

It took only a moment to piece together how he'd found her. Her carriage, of course—was unmistakable and likely parked directly in front of Rosehaven House for all of Grosvenor Square to see. And now he had followed it across the square—in broad daylight, no less—into the home of the very lady his name had recently been linked to. With nursemaids and children milling about, the gossips would already be composing headlines.

"Whatever you came here to learn, Mother," he said, his tone tight, "you should have come to me."

"And would you have answered me, Warwick?" she countered calmly. "You treat me like fragile porcelain. As though the truth might shatter me. I assure you, I'm far stronger than that. As well, you should know."

"I don't want to cause you pain."

"It's far more painful to be kept in the dark about what you and Lady Rosalynd are involved in. Rumor has it you're having an affair. And in Chelsea, of all places." Her lip curled as she spoke the name, her voice dipping into something that almost resembled disdain. There was history in that reaction. Of what sort, I couldn't begin to guess. But clearly, Chelsea struck some hidden nerve.

"Mother!" The duke snapped. "Lady Rosalynd and I are not—"

She arched a perfectly shaped brow. "Of course you aren't. I suspect you're conducting one of your private investigations—this time into Lord Walsh's death. So, sit down, and tell me what you've uncovered."

Steele turned to me with a look of pure exasperation. "I'll take that brandy now."

"Of course, Your Grace." I crossed to the bell pull and gave it a firm tug. When Honeycutt appeared, I relayed the duke's request with a calm I didn't own.

While we waited for Honeycutt to return, the duke spoke, his tone measured. "Lady Rosalynd and I are investigating Lord Walsh's death. It appears he was involved in several unsavory dealings—cheating at cards among them. We've uncovered the names of several individuals, any one of whom might have had motive enough to arrange his murder."

"Isn't Scotland Yard pursuing these leads?" the duchess asked, brows lifting.

"Chief Detective Inspector Dodson hasn't exactly been forthcoming," the duke replied. "Unfortunately, he's become fixated on Nicholas. He recently learned Nicky harbors a tendre for Lady Walsh. And Charles Walsh has publicly accused Julia of murdering his father to clear the way for her marriage to Nicholas, whom he insists is the child's father."

"Heavens," the duchess murmured, a hand drifting to her pearls.

Honeycutt returned with a decanter and a snifter. After placing the tray on a nearby table, he withdrew.

"Should I serve myself?" the duke asked, pointing to the decanter.

I nodded. "Please do."

"As far as I can tell," the duke continued after taking a sip of the spirit, "Dodson isn't investigating other suspects. He's searching for evidence to implicate both Nicky and Lady Walsh."

"And what will he find?" the duchess asked quietly.

I picked up the thread. "Julia insists that she and Lord Nicholas are nothing more than friends. She maintains that the child she's expecting is her husband's. But society is inclined to doubt it—after so many years without children, this sudden pregnancy has tongues wagging. The rumor is that Lord Nicholas paid someone to do away with Walsh so he could marry Julia and claim the child as his own."

"Which he couldn't do," the duke added, "legally or otherwise. Since Julia was married to Walsh, the child is presumed by law to be his."

At that, the duchess exhaled a slow, measured breath, her mind clearly working behind those ice-blue eyes.

But whatever she was about to say would remain a mystery. Because at that very moment, Petunia burst into the room.

"Rosie, it's time for—oh." She halted mid-step, eyes widening as she took in our company. "You have visitors." Then, brightening at the sight of Steele, she added cheerfully, "Hello, Duke!"

"Good morning, Lady Petunia," he replied with a warm smile—far more genial than when they'd first met. Turning to the duchess, he said, "Mother, may I introduce Lady Petunia?"

"What a precious child," the duchess exclaimed, eyes filled with merriment.

Petunia dipped into a curtsy. "Duchess."

"*Your Grace*, poppet. Remember?" I gently corrected.

With a mischievous grin, Petunia turned to Steele's mother and repeated with exaggerated sweetness, "*Your Grace*. Is the duke really your son?"

"He certainly is," the duchess replied, a note of amusement in her voice.

"You don't look anything alike."

"He takes after his father. All three of my sons do."

"You have three sons?"

"I do."

"Petunia, you're being impertinent," I said—though I couldn't quite suppress a smile.

"She's being delightful," the duchess countered, still smiling. "How old are you, my dear?"

"Seven. Do you like fairy cakes?"

"I most certainly do. Let me guess—they're your favorite?"

"They are. The duke's cook baked some for me when I visited him."

The duchess turned a look of quiet wonder toward her son. "Did she really?"

"Don't get any ideas, Mother," he muttered.

"Whatever do you mean?" she asked, all innocence.

At that moment, Mr. Honeycutt appeared in the doorway and bowed with his usual grace. "Luncheon is served, milady."

"Thank you, Mr. Honeycutt," I said with a nod.

"Would you care to join us, Your Grace?" Petunia asked brightly.

"Alas, I cannot, child," the duchess replied with genuine regret. "I've a prior luncheon engagement."

Petunia turned to the duke. "Are *you* free, Your Grace?"

He glanced at his watch. "I believe I am."

"Good. We're having roast beef and potatoes."

"And fairy cakes for dessert?" he asked with a teasing grin.

"Fairy cakes are for teatime," Petunia said with mock severity. "But Cook made Madeira cake. My favorite."

"What a treat that shall be." Then, turning to the duchess, he added, "If there's anything else you'd like to know, Mother, I'll do my best to answer it honestly."

Her Grace gave him a soft look, full of affection. "Thank you, Warwick."

Petunia tugged at his hand. "We'd better get to the dining room before Holly and Ivy steal all the bread rolls."

"Let me guess," he said, following her, "they're your favorite?"

"How did you know?" she asked with an impish grin.

"A wild guess."

As they disappeared through the door, I turned politely to the duchess. "Shall I show you the way out, ma'am?"

"Not just yet." She waited a beat, listening for the footsteps to fade. Then she turned to me, her expression unreadable.

"Whatever you've done to my son," she said quietly, "I heartily approve."

Confused, I shook my head. "I've done nothing, ma'am."

"Oh yes, you have." And with that pithy declaration, she made her way to the door and proceeded down the hallway —leaving behind the faint scent of lavender and something unspoken.

CHAPTER
TWENTY-FIVE

A MATTER OF LEDGERS AND TEA LEAVES

After luncheon, Steele and I withdrew to the morning room to discuss our latest findings. I gestured for him to sit on the settee opposite mine. He declined, choosing instead to hover near the hearth—an embodiment of barely contained restlessness and unspoken thoughts. By now, I'd learned to let him pace. He would settle once his mind had burned off enough energy.

"Lady Farnsworth's tea was a success?" he asked finally.

"I'd classify it as such," I said, smoothing my skirts. "Though some of the truths were swaddled in silk and sugar."

He raised a brow, silent but listening.

I explained how Claire had skillfully guided the conversation toward investments. "Lady Danforth spoke rather freely—after the second round of Darjeeling. She warned her in no uncertain terms to avoid silver mines. Her husband invested thousands and received nothing but regret in return."

Steele frowned. "That tracks with what I learned at White's. Danforth, and Finch as well, revealed that much."

"Do you think Walsh spearheaded the entire scheme?"

"Card cheating, he could manage by himself. But this silver mine scheme was a more complicated affair. A plan had to be devised—where the mine was located, how much money would need to be invested, and arrange for an office to collect correspondence and receive visitors. Walsh did not strike me as a man who could manage something of that magnitude."

"Perhaps he was just the front man," I suggested. "Someone else may have been pulling the strings. One name was mentioned at the tea—an American widow. Mrs. Greystone. She was seen leaving Walsh House at a very late hour. Have you heard of her?"

He nodded slowly. "Quite wealthy. Though the origins of that wealth are entirely speculative. No one seems to know who Mr. Greystone was."

"And yet she maintains an extravagant lifestyle and lives in an opulent Mayfair townhouse."

His expression didn't shift so much as tighten, like a violin string drawn taut.

"I've just finished combing through Walsh's ledgers," he said. "The ones you had delivered to me."

"And?" I prompted.

"There are regular payments from several men. Some greater than others—Danforth, Finch, and Elston among them." He ticked them off on long fingers. "Substantial sums. Repeated over several months. If anyone had reason to silence Walsh, it's those three."

"So they invested in a silver mine that doesn't exist?"

"It appears so."

"But why such large sums?"

"Greed. I suspect Walsh promised an absurd return. All fabrication."

"And the money?"

"Drafts were made out to the Trust. Walsh deposited them into a bank account under the trust's name."

"The one I discovered?"

"No. Another one. It appears legitimate."

"Is that reflected in the ledgers?"

He nodded. "To the tune of over fifty thousand pounds."

"Good heavens."

"Indeed."

"But there's another bank account somewhere that matches the note I found?" I asked.

"It appears so."

"Which bank? And what was its purpose?"

"I have my business manager working on it. Should find out soon. One thing of note, however. Mrs. Greystone's name is notably absent from the accounting books. Not a single mention. No payments. No receipts. Not even a hint."

I frowned. "And yet her name came up at the afternoon tea. Is she involved?"

"Maybe she was too clever to leave a trace. Which leads me to wonder—"

I picked it up. "Could she be the mastermind?"

He nodded once. "A well-connected widow with charm, influence, and discretion? Who would suspect her of double-dealing?"

"But why would Walsh go along with it?"

"Money. His estate was a leaking ship. He needed funds —desperately."

"Charles inherited the leaking ship." A chill crept up my spine. "I wonder if Walsh funneled his ill-gotten gains into an account his son could quietly inherit."

"Perhaps. But Charles inherited a sizable fortune from his mother, so he wouldn't be desperate for money. If managed wisely, he could live comfortably without a penny from his father—though I'm sure he wouldn't have turned it down." He shrugged. "In any case, we'll have to find out."

"And Bellamy?" I asked. "Any chance he had the means? He certainly had a motive."

"Bellamy's a dead end," Steele said. "He's penniless. No way to pay a killer. And he seems genuinely devoted to his mother. The last thing he'd do is risk prison and leave her destitute."

"He must have expenses, though. How does he plan to pay for them?"

"I spoke to his uncle, Osborne. He's taking the boy in hand—hopes to redeem the family name. There's also talk of an understanding with a young lady of means. Substantial dowry."

"So he can squander that as well?"

"I believe he's learned his lesson."

"One can only hope." Although I doubted it.

The mantel clock ticked. Once. Twice. He glanced at his pocket watch. Did it keep better time than our timepiece?

"I must go," he said. "A meeting of the Legislation Committee."

"How's our petition faring?"

"The vote is today," he replied, tucking the watch away. "Don't get your hopes up, Lady Rosalynd. I doubt it will make it out of committee."

"Thank you for supporting it."

"You can try again next year."

"We will. *If* it fails."

He offered a sympathetic smile but offered no further words.

"Regarding the investigation," I said, "we need more than suspicion. We need motive. Proof. And a way to draw Mrs. Greystone out."

He met my eyes—dark, knowing. "Then you'd best invite her to tea."

CHAPTER
TWENTY-SIX

SCHEMES AND SALONS

After the duke departed, I sent Claire a note asking her to come round the next morning for a strategy session. Given her level of curiosity, I knew she'd take the bait. Her reply was delightfully predictable and unmistakably Claire:

In the morning, darling? Why, I'm barely conscious before ten. But for you, yes—I'll be round at eleven. That's the earliest I can manage to make myself presentable.

The following day, Claire swept into the morning room in a rustle of rose-colored skirts, her cheeks flushed from the cold, eyes alight with mischief. The subtle scent of her perfume—something scandalously expensive and vaguely reminiscent of hothouse orchids—trailed behind her as she sank into the settee opposite me with all the theatrical flair of a society actress taking the stage.

"Darling, you look as though you've been pacing all night. How deliciously dramatic. Do say it's something scandalous."

"Only if plotting an ambush counts," I replied. "Though I rather imagine you'll approve. It involves an American widow, suspect investments, and no shortage of guile. Tea?"

Claire's eyes gleamed as she perched delicately on the edge of the settee. "Coffee, if you want me awake. I didn't crawl into bed until four."

"Of course," I said. Once coffee and a light breakfast were served, we settled into our discussion.

"If you recall," I began, handing her a plate, "Mrs. Greystone was mentioned—rather pointedly—at Lady Farnsworth's tea. She was seen leaving Walsh House around midnight several days before his death."

Claire bit into her biscuit with the air of a cat who'd just scented cream. "And you believe Mrs. Greystone was involved?"

"Call it intuition or something more, but yes, I believe she played a part."

"And now you wish to lure her into a trap—upholstered in silk and scented with bergamot. How deliciously subtle."

"My original plan was a quiet tea here," I admitted, passing her a steaming cup. "But that won't do. Between the children and Grandmother—who tends to appear at the most inopportune moments—it would be chaos. Not to mention impossible to conduct any sort of meaningful conversation."

Claire rolled her eyes. "So it falls to me to make something scandalously appropriate out of a social inconvenience."

"Indeed."

She sipped thoughtfully. "A simple tea won't do. Not with someone like Mrs. Greystone. You need something clever. Something layered. What you need, my dear, is a salon."

I arched a brow. "A salon?"

Claire leaned forward, warmed by both firelight and inspiration. "A proper one. Drawing-room discussion, sharp minds and sharper tongues, women only, naturally. An extension of your beloved Society for the Advancement of Women. You'll speak. Oh, don't make that face. You're quite captivating when you're passionate about your causes. Mrs. Greystone will attend just to see who dares to challenge the rules."

I couldn't help a small smile. "You think she'll come?"

"She won't be able to resist. Intellectuals are moths, and I am an exceptionally captivating flame."

Before I could reply, the door opened, and Cosmos stepped inside with the cautious air of a man trespassing into unknown territory. His hair was still damp from the greenhouse, curling slightly at the temples, and he carried a small terracotta pot cradled carefully in both hands.

"Rosalynd," he said, then caught sight of Claire and hesitated. "I didn't realize you had company."

Claire rose with the fluid grace of a prima ballerina and offered a slow, elegant curtsey. "Lord Rosehaven. What a pleasure."

He looked vaguely panicked. "Er—yes. Good morning, Lady Edmunds."

I stood to greet him, unable to help a smile. "What brings you out of your hothouse so early?"

He stepped forward and extended the pot. Nestled within was a delicate spray of tiny white blossoms, their dark green leaves glossy and fine. "It's one of the alpine varieties from Father's collection. I repotted it for you. I thought ... well, your morning room looked rather bare."

Of flowers, he meant. Furnishings were in abundance.

The gesture caught me off guard with its thoughtfulness. I took the pot gently. "Thank you, Cosmos. It's beautiful."

He gave a sheepish nod. "I didn't mean to intrude." His eyes flicked once more to Claire. "I'll leave you to your ... planning."

"Oh, do stay," Claire said, stepping just slightly closer. "I've always had a weakness for alpine flora. So dainty and yet so very resilient."

"They're hardy by necessity," he said, shifting awkwardly.

"I do admire necessary hardiness," she murmured, her eyes full of wicked amusement.

Cosmos flushed to the roots of his hair.

"Claire," I said sharply, slicing through the charged moment like a blade through silk.

She turned to me with a look of mock innocence—lips demure, eyes dancing—and then faced Cosmos once more. "Well then, thank you for the visit. Do enjoy your greenhouse."

Cosmos gave a strangled sort of nod and retreated, nearly tripping over the edge of the rug on his way out.

The moment the door clicked shut behind him, I set the pot down and turned on Claire. "Must you toy with him?"

"I wasn't toying," Claire said, serenely reclaiming her seat. "Merely appreciating. He's rather lovely, in an absentminded, scholarly sort of way."

"Lovely?" I echoed, incredulous. "Whatever are you talking about?"

"You wouldn't notice as you're his sister. But he is. Quite striking, really. Those curls like velvet, the shade of aged wine. And those eyes—stormy and distant, like the sea just before it breaks." She paused, then added with a dreamy sigh, "And he hides a surprisingly fit physique beneath all that tweed. Like a Grecian statue who got lost in an herbarium."

"Honestly, Claire," I muttered. "Where do you come up with these notions? He's not like other men. He's quiet. Gentle. Entirely uninterested in romantic pursuits."

Claire raised one perfect brow. "You mean he's uninterested in women."

"I mean, he's uninterested in anyone who doesn't photosynthesize."

She gave a soft hum of amusement, clearly unconvinced. "You misjudge him."

"No, I don't," I said, the edge easing from my voice. "A woman like you would turn him inside out."

Claire exhaled through her nose, then nodded solemnly. "Very well. I shan't flirt. I'll be a sister. Or a cousin. Second cousin, perhaps. Third, if that's less threatening. You have my word."

"Thank you."

With the awkward moment passed, Claire's attention returned to the task at hand with mercurial enthusiasm. "Now then, this salon. We'll hold it, let's see." She tapped a delicate finger against her lips. "Tuesday afternoon. You'll introduce the theme—*The Role of Women in Financial Autonomy: A Civilized Discussion*—and I shall supply the sherry and the sparkle."

"I can already hear my grandmother's cane striking the floorboards in protest."

"All the more reason to make it unforgettable," Claire said, eyes alight. "We'll fill the room with ladies who have something to say and no one who dares tell them not to say it. We'll give Mrs. Greystone the spotlight—then watch what shadows she casts."

I lifted my teacup in salute. "To schemes and salons."

Claire clinked hers against mine. "And to uncovering whatever secrets bloom in the shade."

CHAPTER
TWENTY-SEVEN

VELVET AND VENEER

Lady Claire's drawing room had been transformed into a showcase of genteel rebellion—velvet cushions in sapphire and garnet scattered across chaise lounges, sherry gleaming in cut-crystal decanters, and a fire crackling in the hearth as if in support of the cause. The scent of lilies and bergamot perfumed the air, mingling with the sharper, unspoken notes of rivalry and ambition.

I arrived early, as agreed, wearing violet silk with a high collar and jet buttons—subdued, but striking enough to suggest purpose. Today was not about fashion, but message. I was here to speak, to persuade, to rattle the gilded cage just enough to make the occupants notice the bars.

The guest list had been chosen with care—and, in some cases, cunning. Ladies Danforth, Finch, and Farnsworth arrived in a tight cluster, all curious glances and thin smiles. Mrs. Greystone entered shortly thereafter, wrapped in dove-grey satin with silver trim, her every movement deliberate. She chose a seat near the hearth, observing the room with the detachment of someone assessing a business opportunity.

From the Society for the Advancement of Women came our strongest voices: Lady Whitworth, upright and sharp-eyed; Lady Sheffield, whose wry remarks often disguised deeper strategies; and Miss Moore, the young heiress with a mind like a forge and a bank account to match. She settled into her chair with an eagerness that was encouraging and dangerous.

Claire, a vision in peacock silk and sapphires, presided over the affair with her usual mix of practiced charm and barely veiled delight in the possibility of scandal. She moved through the room like a conductor, guiding everyone with a raised brow, a light touch, or a well-timed quip. Once everyone had been seated and offered refreshments, she clapped her hands with gentle finality.

"Ladies," she began, her voice warm and lilting, "thank you for braving the weather, your calendars, and—dare I say—the weight of public expectation to join us. This afternoon's salon is held under the auspices of the Society for the Advancement of Women, and it is my great pleasure to introduce our guest speaker—Lady Rosalynd Rosehaven. She has, as many of you know, been delightfully persistent in her advocacy for women's rights, and I, for one, cannot wait to be provoked."

Laughter followed—some genuine, some politely restrained.

I rose, smoothing my notes more from habit than necessity. My words were already with me.

"I thank Lady Claire for the invitation and the generous introduction. Today's subject is one that touches every woman in this room, whether directly or through those we care for—financial independence."

A subtle hush fell, curiosity sharpening into attention.

"We speak often of virtue and duty, and somewhat less of marriage's true cost. Rarely do we discuss income or investment, though these are the levers by which lives are shaped—or ruined. Dependence on a father, brother, or husband is not simply inconvenient. It's a gamble. And far too often, we are left to pay the price."

Lady Danforth gave a soft snort and set down her teacup with a clink. "But what are we to do about it, Lady Rosalynd? The law does not grant us financial independence. We cannot open a bank account, we cannot sign a contract, we cannot even run a business without pretending some man is behind it."

A murmur of agreement rippled through the group.

"Because under the law, we are not individuals. We are dependents—first of our fathers, then of our husbands. Even widows are expected to hand the reins to a son or male trustee. A woman in England cannot open a bank account in her own name. She cannot take out a loan. She cannot file suit. And if she dares run a business, she must do so under a man's name or hide behind a fictitious one."

Lady Finch frowned. "Even if she funds it herself?"

"Even then," I said. "The Married Women's Property Acts were a step forward, but not a leap. Until we are recognized as legal entities, not extensions of our husbands or brothers, we will remain—financially and legally—at the mercy of others."

There was a silence after that, the kind that settled not in discomfort, but in understanding. A shared recognition of the quiet, invisible battleground we all navigated daily.

Building on that emotion, I continued, "We are taught to entrust our futures to men. And some are worthy of that trust. But when they are not—when they are careless, or corrupt, or simply indifferent—we are left with little recourse. Autonomy without resources is no autonomy at all."

Miss Moore nodded firmly, her expression alight, and a glint of agreement showed in Lady Sheffield's eyes.

Lady Barlow, seated near the window in a soft rose-colored gown, shifted delicately and placed a gloved hand over the gentle swell of her stomach. "But surely the law exists to protect us, does it not?" she asked, her voice light but earnest. "To ensure our husbands provide for us and our children. Isn't that the point of all these arrangements —to safeguard the family?"

Several heads turned in her direction, a few nodding faintly.

I offered her a smile—gentle, but tinged with gravity. "Yes, Lady Barlow, that is what we are told; the law guards our welfare. That it spares us the burden of responsibility. But in truth, it also strips us of agency. Protection can be a gilded cage."

She blinked, uncertain.

"I've seen too many women 'protected' into poverty," I continued. "Their fortunes lost through a husband's recklessness. Their inheritance redirected to male heirs. Their homes mortgaged, their jewels sold, their children left dependent on the goodwill of relatives. And they can do nothing—because the law that shields them also binds them."

Lady Barlow's hand stilled on her belly, her expression softening with thought.

"I would never argue against safeguarding one's child," I added. "But I would ask—why must our security be tethered to the choices of men? Why must we be rendered powerless in order to be 'safe'?"

A soft rustle of silk drew our attention as Mrs. Greystone, seated with unassuming elegance near the hearth, lifted her teacup with a knowing smile. "I daresay I've managed well enough," she said, her American accent lending her words a crisp confidence. "The law may not favor women, but that hasn't stopped me from keeping a close eye on my investments."

Lady Danforth arched a brow. "You've taken control of your own accounts?"

"I have," she replied smoothly. "Mr. Greystone left me a tidy sum. No children, no meddling in-laws, and no trust to bind my hands. I learned early that money in a woman's name may be rare—but money under her control is rarer still. So I studied the markets. I made discreet inquiries. And I placed my trust not in the law, but in ledgers."

Claire leaned forward, eyes gleaming. "But how? Aren't there legal barriers?"

"Oh, certainly," Mrs. Greystone said, taking a delicate sip. "That's why I have a business manager who knows how to keep my name off the front page and my signature off the wrong forms. I may not own things publicly, but I control them privately. There's always a way, if one's determined enough, and has a reliable clerk or two."

I smiled faintly. "So long as you're clever, and they are utterly discreet."

"Precisely," she said. "It isn't freedom, not really. But it's a kind of power. And sometimes, that's the more useful currency."

Lady Danforth leaned forward, her brow furrowed slightly. "But how do you find such a man? And how do you place your trust in him?"

Mrs. Greystone's smile didn't falter, though it cooled a degree. "You don't *find* such a man, Lady Danforth. You *choose* him—carefully. And you never place blind trust in anyone."

She set her teacup aside and adjusted her gloves with practiced elegance. "I select the investments. I study companies, shipping lines, mining prospects—whatever shows promise. I do the research. My financial manager merely executes the trades and monitors the markets."

There was a pause as several ladies exchanged glances.

"I also pay him a share of the profits," she added, smoothing her skirts. "So he can invest on his own behalf as well. He's independently wealthy now, but remains in my employ for one very good reason: he knows I understand value—of stock, of strategy, and of loyalty."

Claire gave a low whistle under her breath, drawing a withering look from Lady Finch.

Mrs. Greystone went on, her tone silk-wrapped steel. "And he also knows that if he ever betrays my trust—if even a single farthing disappears unaccounted for—I will make him regret it. Financially, socially, and, if necessary, legally."

Her smile returned, genteel and untroubled. "But of course, we've never had a problem."

Before anyone could speak, a voice piped up from the corner. Lady Tinsley, who had shown little interest in finance but never missed a whiff of scandal.

"But what about Walsh's silver mine?" she asked with faux innocence, her eyes gleaming. "We heard you visited him at rather *late* hours, Mrs. Greystone."

A few fans fluttered, and a whisper of breathless anticipation rustled through the room.

Mrs. Greystone turned her head slowly toward Lady

Tinsley, her smile sharpening by degrees. "Indeed, I did. And had your informant been closer to the door, they might've heard what I actually said."

The room quieted.

"I went to Walsh not for investment," she continued, her voice cool and crisp as a dry wind, "but to warn him. What he was doing was fraud, plain and simple. And he was ruining lives—widows, spinsters, married women with no control over their dowries. He'd convinced their fathers, brothers, husbands, they would gain a fortune. I told him that if he did not cease and withdraw the scheme, I would go to the authorities myself."

She leaned back with the easy poise of a woman unbothered by judgment. "And I meant it. I had evidence enough to prove the mine didn't exist. Had he not died, I would have seen him pay."

There was a pause. No one reached for their tea.

Then Claire let out a quiet, impressed, "Well."

Mrs. Greystone glanced around the room, her gaze unflinching. "Let that be a lesson, ladies. If you must trade in whispers, at least make sure the truth speaks louder than gossip."

That earned her a smattering of applause, mostly from our Society members, whose eyes glittered with something far keener than amusement.

Claire, ever attuned to the currents of a room, rose gracefully, her smile bright as cut crystal. "Well," she said, her voice lifting the mood with practiced ease, "I believe Lady Rosalynd and Mrs. Greystone have given us much to consider. I suggest we refresh our glasses and allow the conversation to unfold naturally."

A ripple of agreement followed. The tension, though not entirely gone, eased as cups were refilled, fans resumed their gentle fluttering, and talk shifted toward the more familiar terrain of who was dancing with whom, whose cook had run off, and whether Lady Pelham's third daughter was truly engaged or merely hopeful.

As I stood near the sideboard, reaching for a fresh pot of tea, I felt a presence beside me.

Mrs. Greystone.

Her voice was low, meant only for me. "You handled that with admirable composure, Lady Rosalynd. And conviction. You speak of change, not as a dream, but as something attainable."

I turned to face her, warmed and steadied by her words. "Thank you. But it's not something I can achieve alone."

She gave a wry smile. "Fortunately, you don't have to. I'd like to offer my support—particularly with the Society for the Advancement of Women. I believe I can be of use."

I returned her smile with genuine pleasure. "I would be honoured. I'll send you notice of our next meeting. You would be most welcomed."

Her gloved hand brushed my arm—a small gesture, but one filled with significance. Then she slipped away, already half-absorbed into another circle of conversation, leaving behind the scent of bergamot and the quiet promise of alliance.

As the afternoon waned, voices softened, chairs shifted, and the clinking of cups grew sparse. The sharp edges of earlier conversation had dulled into the hum of gossip and gentle laughter. One by one, the ladies made their farewells, trailing lavender perfume and murmured thanks.

I stood near the window, watching the last carriage pull away, when Claire joined me, a crystal glass of watered wine in her hand.

"Well," she said lightly, "that was livelier than our usual discussions about lace imports and unwed cousins."

I gave a soft laugh. "I hadn't planned on igniting a revolution over tea."

Claire sipped and gave me a sidelong glance. "And yet, here we are. Mrs. Greystone, no less. I must say, I didn't expect her to be quite so formidable."

"She's exactly what we need," I said. "She sees the battlefield clearly. And she's willing to fight smart."

Claire leaned against the windowsill, thoughtful. "Do you think the others were truly listening? Or simply enjoying the spectacle?"

"Both," I said. "But sometimes spectacle is the wedge. It makes space for the seed to be planted."

She smiled at that, then fell silent for a beat. "You're doing something real, Rosalynd. I hope you know that."

I looked at her—truly looked—and saw not just my friend, but my ally. "So are you."

She grinned. "Of course I am. I brought the sherry."

I laughed, the kind that lingers in the chest even after it fades.

We stood like that a moment longer, two women at the edge of something uncertain but undeniable.

Change was coming—whether society welcomed it or not—and I for one intended to meet it head-on.

CHAPTER
TWENTY-EIGHT

BITTER INFUSION

The scent of lilies and bergamot still clung to me when the door to Rosehaven House opened—not by a footman, but by Mr. Honeycutt himself. That alone was enough to set my nerves on edge.

He stood in the threshold with grave composure, his gloved hands folded before him, his expression unusually solemn. Without a word, he stepped aside to admit me. The door closed behind with a solid click, the sound echoing through the silence like a verdict.

I had only just begun to unpin my hat when I caught the look in his eyes—gentle, steady, and burdened with something far heavier than words.

"Milady," he said quietly. "There's been ... news."

I froze, my hand suspended mid-motion. "What sort of news?"

He met my gaze with calm sorrow. "It's Lord Walsh, milady. Lord Charles Walsh. He's—he's dead."

"Dead?" The word struck like a stone, hollowing the air

between us. For a moment, all I could hear was the ticking of the long-case clock in the corridor and the distant rumble of carriage wheels outside.

"Yes, milady. Word arrived just a short time ago. He collapsed in his study at Walsh House."

I moved past him into the morning room, heart hammering in my chest like a warning bell. The space felt too still, too bright, as though the room itself was holding its breath.

"How?" I asked, my voice thinner than I intended. I didn't know what I feared more—a tragic accident, or something far worse.

Mr. Honeycutt followed and closed the door behind us. "They found him slumped over his desk," he said. "A cup of tea in his hand."

I stared at him, stunned. Tea.

Julia had sent him a parcel of her special blend—the same served at the reading of the will. But I shouldn't jump to conclusions. Charles had a weak heart. It could have been natural.

Before I could respond, a sharp knock sounded at the door, followed immediately by a second, more insistent one. Mr. Honeycutt, already tense, moved to answer it.

Inspector Dodson stood in the hall, hat in hand, grim purpose written across his face. Two uniformed constables trailed behind him like shadows. As they made their entrance, Mr. Honeycutt quietly slipped away.

"Lady Rosalynd," Dodson said by way of greeting, inclining his head with what passed for respect.

"Inspector," I replied cautiously, my stomach tightening. "What brings you—?"

"I'm here for Lady Julia Walsh," he said without

preamble, retrieving a document from inside his jacket. "She is to be taken into custody on suspicion of murder."

For one breathless moment, I felt the ground tilt beneath me. But collapsing would not do. I straightened my spine and forced my voice to remain steady. "You cannot be serious."

"Indeed, I am," Dodson continued, his voice clipped and certain. "Lord Charles Walsh died shortly after consuming tea laced with foxglove. The amount present was enough to stop a man's heart. The cook confirmed the tea was brewed from the custom blend Lady Julia Walsh sent him. We examined the remaining leaves. There were signs of foxglove."

Julia had poisoned Charles. Or so he would have us believe.

"Signs are not proof, Inspector," I said, my voice low but cutting. "What time did Charles die?"

"His body was discovered at noon when the butler entered the study to announce luncheon."

I glanced at the mantel clock. "It's five o'clock now. No formal analysis could have been conducted in so short a time. You're relying on assumptions and haste to condemn an innocent woman—and one expecting a child at that."

Dodson's mouth pulled taut. "The presence of foxglove—"

"You don't know that's what it was. It takes an expert to identify a plant." I'd learned that much from Cosmos. "This is not justice. It's spectacle. If you drag Lady Julia from this house without proper cause, you will answer for it."

A new voice cut through the air, cool and deliberate. "I believe the lady has a point."

Steele stepped into the room like a shadow cast by judgment itself. He wore no hat, no coat, no gloves, only the implacable expression of a man who had heard enough and would tolerate no more. The air shifted around him, taut and breathless, as if even the house itself knew to fall silent in his presence.

His eyes swept the room, taking in the constables, the paper in Dodson's hand. And, more than likely, the pallor in my face.

"What precisely is your business here, Inspector?" he asked, his voice low and cold. "Because unless you have something more than innuendo and intimidation, I suggest you remove your boots from Lady Rosalynd's carpet."

Dodson's spine straightened, his chin lifting as though he could shield himself with protocol alone. "I am here on official business," he said, voice taut. "To execute a lawful arrest warrant for Lady Julia Walsh, on suspicion of murder."

Steele's gaze didn't waver. "Based on?"

"The victim—Lord Charles Walsh—was found dead in his study. A teacup in hand. The blend came from Lady Julia. Preliminary examination of the leaves suggests the presence of foxglove."

Steele stepped closer, not looming, but somehow reducing the space between them to something razor-thin. "*Suggests*, Inspector?" he said, each syllable polished and exacting. "A suggestion is not evidence, especially when a coroner has yet to perform the post-mortem, and toxicological results are days away. So, what exactly do you have? A cook's recollection? A leaf you *believe* came from foxglove? Come, Inspector, you are no expert on poisonous plants."

"I have experience with such things," Dodson declared.

"Experience is *not* evidence." Steele towered over Dodson, an intimidation tactic he excelled at. "You arrive at a noblewoman's residence, flanked by constables, and attempt to arrest a grieving, pregnant widow on the strength of observation and experience?"

"We found the remaining tea in the packet Lady Julia sent—"

"*Allegedly sent*," Steele interrupted, his tone dangerous in its quiet precision. "You have motive and supposition. What you do not have is proof."

Dodson's jaw tightened. "This is not a matter of speculation, Your Grace. The warrant was properly reviewed and signed by Magistrate Harwood this morning." With clipped formality, he held out the document in his hand to Steele. "You'll find it in order."

Steele took it without a word, unfolded the paper, and scanned its contents. His expression remained unreadable, though the muscle ticking in his jaw betrayed the storm simmering just beneath.

"I see," he said quietly, refolding the warrant with deliberate care. "A legal instrument hastily drawn, based on evidence not yet confirmed, naming a woman with no history of violence and no means to flee." He handed it back to Dodson. "What you have, Inspector," the duke bit out, "is an official document. What you *lack* is judgment."

Dodson bristled. "I have the authority of the Crown."

"And I," Steele said coolly, "have the means to see that Lady Julia Walsh remains under protection, in a secure environment befitting her condition—not paraded through the streets for the satisfaction of gossip and spectacle."

After a long, brittle pause, Dodson gave a stiff nod. "Very well. She may remain at Rosehaven House—under guard." He turned to the constables. "Post yourselves at the front and rear entrances. Inside the house." He directed a scornful gaze at Steele. "We wouldn't want to cause a scandal."

"Agreed," Steele said, his voice like cut glass. "But let me be clear. If Lady Julia Walsh is harmed, distressed, or placed under any further public scrutiny before your evidence can hold up in court, you will answer for it."

Dodson's eyes narrowed, but he said nothing more. With a jerk of his head, he signaled to the constables, then turned on his heel.

But the inspector had one more salvo to hurl before leaving. In dramatic fashion, he paused in the doorway as Steele and I both faced him.

"You're wasting your influence, Your Grace," he said, his tone cutting. "You'd be better served protecting your own family."

Steele's shoulders tensed. "What exactly do you mean by that?"

Dodson gave a tight smile. "I have sufficient grounds to issue a warrant for Lord Nicholas. A witness from a low tavern in Spitalfields claims to have seen him speaking with a man well known to the Yard—one who'd slit a throat for sixpence and not lose a wink of sleep over it."

My blood turned cold. The implication was clear. Lord Nicholas had hired a killer to murder Lord Walsh.

"That witness is being vetted, of course," Dodson continued as he arranged his bowler hat on his head with deliberate precision. "We're trying to locate Lord Nicholas. He appears to have disappeared."

Steele's voice was like flint striking stone. "If he has gone to ground, it may be because he's being hunted by someone who wants this case closed before the truth comes to light."

"Or it may be because he has something to hide." Dodson adjusted the cuffs of his gloves with exaggerated calm. "If you happen to find him before we do, Your Grace, kindly let him know we're coming."

And with that parting shot, he made his exit. Moments later, the front door closed with a muffled thud.

As silence pressed in, I faced Steele. "That was very well done," I said aloud, my voice steady, cool—the sort one might use when commenting on a well-executed speech in Parliament, not a personal triumph witnessed from a breath away.

But privately, traitorously, the truth flared within me. *He'd been magnificent.*

Not just his strategy or poise, though those alone would merit the word. It was *him*. The quiet force of his presence. The sharp edge of his mind. The way he shielded Julia—a woman he barely knew—without seeking thanks or recognition. I saw it now, all of it, and the revelation left me breathless.

And frightened.

Because I had begun to think of him not merely as a partner in enquiry or necessity, but as something more. And that was a risk I hadn't accounted for.

"I know the law, Lady Rosalynd," he said quietly, cutting into my thoughts.

"You held off Dodson today, but I doubt he'll give up," I said.

"*We* held him off," he corrected. "I heard what you said to him. You were holding your own." He drew in a breath, steadying himself. "But you're right. Dodson won't stop. Not only is he under pressure to solve Walsh's murder, but he sees this investigation as an opportunity to wound me."

"Because you tried to have him demoted."

He nodded. "Revenge is a powerful motivator. He'll stop at nothing. And that means he'll do everything he can to implicate Nicky. He knows the way to get to him is through Lady Walsh. In her condition, she might very well confess to something she hasn't done—especially if she believes it could protect her unborn child."

He paused, the line of his jaw tightening. "Hanover must be informed. He'll know what measures can be taken to safeguard Lady Walsh. The sooner, the better."

"I'll send a footman with a note."

He inclined his head.

"Do you think Dodson actually has evidence against Nicholas?"

"If he doesn't, he can fabricate it. Not the murder weapon, but a witness? That's another matter entirely. He'll have no trouble finding someone willing to lie to stay out of prison." He gestured toward the streak of white in his dark hair. "A glimpse of this under a hat, and a thug might swear he saw Nicky just to earn Dodson's favor."

A discreet knock at the drawing room door interrupted us, and Mr. Honeycutt appeared once more. "Forgive me, milady, Lady Walsh has need of you."

"Yes, of course." I glanced at the duke. "I must go."

"One more thing before you do," the duke said.

I glanced at our butler. "Please tell Lady Walsh I'll be with her in a moment."

After he departed, closing the door behind him, I turned to the duke. "Yes?"

"See to her, of course," Steele said. "But don't linger. There's something else that needs to be done. Today."

"What?"

"You need to visit Walsh House. Speak with the staff. We need to know exactly what happened from the moment that packet of tea arrived."

"The tea Lady Julia sent Charles?"

He nodded. "Who received it? Who handled it? Was it stored or opened? Who brewed it, and did anyone else have access to it before it was steeped? And most importantly—" His gaze sharpened. "Who was present in the house between the tea's arrival and the moment Charles Walsh drank it?"

I frowned. "You think it was someone in the house?"

"It has to be," he said quietly.

His certainty sent a chill along my spine. His implication was clear. Someone at Walsh House had murdered Charles.

"After I attend to Julia," I said, already moving, "I'll go to Walsh House and find out what happened."

He gave a single nod, but his eyes followed me to the door—watching, calculating, already several steps ahead.

I paused on the threshold. "And what will you do?"

He didn't hesitate. "Find Nicky."

For a moment, I stood there, caught in the silence between us. His expression gave nothing away, but something in his gaze held fast to mine—steady, unwavering. I nodded once, then turned and left, the echo of his words lingering in my mind long after I'd gone.

CHAPTER
TWENTY-NINE

A HOUSE REMEMBERS

Julia sat on the edge of a chaise, wrapped in a delicate shawl, her eyes glassy and unfocused. She didn't look up when I entered, didn't stir when I crossed to her side. Only the fine tremble in her fingertips betrayed that she was aware of me at all.

I sat beside her and took her hand gently. "Julia, darling, what is it?" I asked, though I already knew. Dodson's arrival, she had to have heard of it. Word must have traveled like wildfire up the stairs to her room. The threat of arrest had taken its toll. But she needed to say it, to give shape to the fear hollowing her out.

At the sound of my voice, her chin quivered. "They'll take me away," she whispered, barely audible. "They'll take me, and I'll lose everything." Her hand curled protectively around her stomach. "I'll lose my child."

A tear traced down her cheek. I caught it with my thumb. "You will not be moved, Julia. You are staying here in Rosehaven House. Steele and I saw to that."

"They've posted police officers downstairs," she said in a strangled whisper.

I couldn't very well deny it. She already knew. "Two constables. They're here to keep you safe, not drag you off. You needn't speak to them, or even see them at all."

She gave a shuddering breath. "But how will I manage? I need to eat. For the baby's sake, if not for my own."

I reached for her hand again, wrapping it firmly in mine. "And you shall. Every tray of food, every need, will come straight to you. All you have to do is rest, Julia. You must regain your strength. Let me carry the weight of this. You've carried enough."

Her hand closed over mine with more strength than I expected. "I didn't kill him, Rosalynd."

I met her gaze, unflinching. "I know you didn't."

The tension in her body eased as she drew a steadying breath, the kind one takes when hope, however faint, begins to return.

~

THE JOURNEY across Mayfair to Walsh House passed in silence. I sat in the corner of the carriage, my thoughts racing with the one question that refused to be stilled.

Who had killed Charles?

It had to be someone with access to Walsh House. Steele was right about that. Only such a person could have tampered with the tea packet Julia had sent. Of her innocence, I had no doubt. She simply didn't have it in her to commit murder.

And yet, there was one fact that could condemn her.

She had access to foxglove.

Cosmos had told me he encountered her during her

garden walk on Saturday morning. Upon their return, he'd shown her the specimen in his study. If Dodson ever learned that detail, it would be more than enough to justify a second warrant—this time with damning evidence in hand. And if that happened, I feared we wouldn't be able to stop him.

Which meant I needed answers—and quickly. Somewhere inside Walsh House lay the truth. I intended to follow the trail wherever it led.

Walsh House wore its mourning like a shroud. The windows, though curtained, seemed darker than usual, the once-pristine façade dulled by soot and shadow. The brass knocker had been removed from the front door, in keeping with custom—a silent emblem of death within. But without it, there was no dignified way to announce myself.

I hesitated only a moment before raising my gloved hand and rapping firmly on the door. The sound was inelegant, far too loud in the still evening air—but effective. Within moments, the door swung open, and a harried footman blinked out at me.

"Milady," he said, startled, and stepped back at once to admit me.

I crossed the threshold into a house heavy with silence. The air inside was thick with the scent of extinguished fires and fading lilies. Every footstep felt too loud, too alive. Grief clung to the walls—but so did secrets.

I intended to draw them into the light.

"Is Mr. Anstruther at home?" I asked.

"Yes, milady," the footman replied, lowering his voice instinctively. "He's in the steward's office."

"Fetch him, please. Tell him I'd appreciate a word. In private."

The young man bowed and disappeared down the corridor.

Moments later, Mr. Anstruther appeared, his step brisk despite the weight of mourning that hung in the house. His expression registered surprise, then something gentler—recognition, perhaps, or quiet approval.

"My lady," he said with a respectful nod. "I trust Lady Walsh is ... managing?"

"She's resting. I've come on her behalf," I said softly. "And I need your help."

He hesitated only a moment before nodding. "This way, if you please."

He led me through a narrow passage and into a small sitting room off the servants' hall, modest but tidy, with the faint scent of polish and pipe smoke still lingering in the air. He closed the door behind us.

"Before we begin," I said, lowering my voice, "who is currently in the house?"

"Only the household staff, my lady," he replied without hesitation. "The family solicitor departed earlier this afternoon, and the physician has already seen Lady Lucretia. She's taken to her chambers and hasn't spoken with anyone beyond her maid."

"No other visitors? No one calling under false pretenses?"

"None," he said with quiet certainty. "No one's crossed the threshold who doesn't belong."

I nodded. "Good. Then we may speak freely."

He waited, hands clasped behind his back, patient and ready.

"I need to know what happened yesterday after the tea packet arrived," I said. "Who received it? Who handled it? Was it opened or moved? And most importantly, who brewed the tea and who was in this house between the time it was delivered and the moment it was served?"

Mr. Anstruther gave a slow nod, clearly sorting through the sequence of events.

"The parcel arrived just after noon," he began. "I had just brought brandy to the study for Lord Walsh and Mr. Heller when the doorbell rang. I answered it myself. A footman dressed in Rosehaven livery handed me a small brown-paper parcel, addressed to Lord Walsh in Lady Julia's hand."

Of course, he would recognize it—he'd served her long enough to know.

"I took it straight to the study. Mr. Heller was seated near the hearth; Lord Walsh behind his desk. I placed the parcel before him and mentioned it was from Her Ladyship. He thanked me and set it aside without opening it."

"Did either of them touch it?"

"Not that I saw. I left the room shortly after."

"And then?"

"That's less certain," he admitted. "I didn't return to the study again until just before four, when Lord Walsh retired to his chambers. By then, the parcel was gone. I assumed he'd taken it upstairs or passed it along to the staff."

"Who found it next?"

"Cook told me it was brought to her by Elsie—the second housemaid—just after six."

"And did Lord Walsh give it to her directly?"

"No, my lady. She found it in the morning room, sitting on a side table. It had been unwrapped but was still sealed. A note was pinned to it: '*To be used exclusively for Lord Walsh's tea.*'"

"Did you recognize the handwriting?"

"No, milady. I'm not familiar with His Lordship's hand."

I frowned. "So between noon and six, the packet vanished from the study, reappeared in the morning room, and was then brought to the kitchen?"

"Exactly so."

I noted the sequence carefully in my small notebook. Then looked back to him. "Who brewed the tea?"

"Cook. Lord Walsh called for tea this morning while working in his study. He hadn't had any the day before—only brandy with Mr. Heller, then burgundy with his supper. For breakfast, he requested coffee."

"So the tea made from the packet was brewed only once—this morning?"

He nodded. "Just before ten. Elsie brought it up on a tray."

A silence fell between us as the implications settled. Six hours unaccounted for. And a tea packet that changed hands without a witness.

"Thank you, Mr. Anstruther. I'd like to speak with Cook now."

"She's in the kitchen, my lady. It's nearly supper. She'll be hard-pressed to leave her post."

"Of course."

He led me down the hall, where the warm scent of yeast and rosemary greeted us. We found Cook at the long table, rolling pastry with firm precision. She looked up as we entered, wiping her hands on her apron.

"Lady Rosalynd," she said, her surprise softened by concern. "I reckon you're here about the tea."

I nodded. "Tell me everything."

She leaned back against the table, arms folded. "Elsie brought it in. I didn't open it right away—just slipped it into a caddy to keep it fresh and set it on the shelf with the others. When I opened it this morning, it looked fine. Crushed leaves. Smelled herbal. Not unpleasant."

"But it could've been tampered with."

She hesitated. "Aye. Could've been. Easy enough to open the parchment, sprinkle something in, and wrap it up again. Wouldn't take two minutes."

"Did anyone else touch it?"

"Not that I know of. But it wasn't locked up. We don't treat tea like it's diamonds. Anyone could've reached it between the time Elsie handed it over and when I brewed it."

I thought of the narrow staircases, the servants' corridors, the familiar rhythm of a household in motion. Trusted routines. Familiar faces. Too trusted.

"So the suspects are limited to those within the house," I murmured.

"Or visitors," Mr. Anstruther reminded me gently.

"Yes. Indeed." I turned to Cook. "The tea—has it all been taken?"

"Yes, milady. That inspector—Dodson—took it." Her look made clear what she thought of him.

I thanked her and asked to speak with Elsie, who confirmed what had been said. With that done, I made my way back toward the front entrance. It was nearing seven. My family would be wondering what had kept me away so long. But I had one last question.

"Mr. Anstruther," I said, as he helped me into my coat. "Do you happen to know Mr. Heller's address?"

"43 Duke Street." He hesitated. "You're not planning to go there alone, are you, milady?"

"No," I said. "But I intend to share that information." After a moment's pause, I asked, "Was he notified of Lord Walsh's passing?"

"I sent a footman early this afternoon, but no one was at home. We left word that an urgent matter required his attention."

I stepped into the growing dusk, the weight of unanswered questions heavier than before. My trusted coachman waited at the curb. I climbed into the carriage, and the door closed with a soft thud.

As we rolled back toward Rosehaven House, I leaned into the shadows, reviewing every detail I had gathered.

A vanished tea packet. A visiting cousin. A note no one could verify.

And a house full of people. Maybe one with something to lose.

CHAPTER
THIRTY

RETURN TO ROSEHAVEN HOUSE

The carriage rolled to a smooth halt beneath the portico of Rosehaven House just as the final blush of daylight faded from the sky. I descended without assistance, my thoughts still churning with unanswered questions and the quiet menace of what I had discovered at Walsh House. The front door opened before I could lift a hand to knock.

Mr. Honeycutt—ever precise, ever composed—greeted me with his customary bow. "Lady Rosalynd. Welcome home."

I handed him my coat, gloves, and hat. Mindful of the police officer present, I simply asked, "How is Lady Walsh faring?"

"She remains in her rooms, milady. Her supper was taken up not long ago. Our housekeeper reports that she ate a modest amount and has retired with a book."

"Has she received any visitors?"

"Mr. Hanover."

I gave a small nod, relieved. Julia's solicitor would do his utmost to see justice done. "Thank you, Mr. Honeycutt."

With no time to waste, I crossed the hall and made for the morning room. Its curtains were drawn tight, something I appreciated as the evening had turned quite chilly. Moving to the writing desk, I quickly retrieved pen, ink, and a sheet of thick cream paper. With measured strokes, I began to write:

Steele,

I've returned from Walsh House and have learned much—though far from everything.

The tea packet was delivered to the study while Edwin Heller was present. Mr. Anstruther, the Walsh House butler, placed it on Charles's desk. It disappeared from the study and reappeared hours later in the morning room, where a housemaid retrieved it and brought it to Cook. The note attached was in an unfamiliar hand and directed that the tea was only to be brewed for Charles's tea.

Cook confirms it was not locked away but simply kept on a shelf. Anyone could have tampered with it before it was brewed this morning.

Also of note: Mr. Heller has not returned since his visit and could not be found at his Duke Street lodgings.

Please come as soon as you can so we can discuss what I learned. I will wait for you, no matter the hour.

—R.

I folded the letter, wrote Steele's name on the envelope, and pressed my seal to the wax with a firm hand. The moment it cooled, I rang the bell to summon Honeycutt.

As soon as he appeared, I handed it to him. "Please see that it's delivered immediately."

"Of course, milady." He bowed. "Supper is being served."

"Thank you, Mr. Honeycutt." I allowed a small smile to form on my lips. "I don't know if I've said this enough. But you are a treasure."

"Milady." I thought I detected a blush on his cheeks as he bowed once more.

After smoothing my skirts, I made my way to the dining room where my family was already gathered. The chandelier glowed overhead, casting warm light over porcelain and polished silver.

Chrissie was positively glowing—chattering about her debut with all the youthful delight of someone who had never tasted real worry. Petunia listened wide-eyed, soaking it all in, while Cosmos presided at the head of the table like a general surveying his troops.

I took my seat and offered a smile, joining the conversation without revealing the storm that churned beneath my calm facade.

Talk turned to gowns and dance cards, to whether Chrissie might waltz with Viscount Darrow or catch the eye of a certain baron's eldest son.

"You've been quiet, Rosalynd," Cosmos observed after the fish course was served. "Anything I ought to know about?"

I lifted my wineglass and smiled. "Only that I've had enough scandal this week to last me through Chrissie's entire season. I intend to be as dull as toast from here on out."

The children laughed, as children often do when they think something is a joke, and the conversation moved on. But my thoughts remained fixed on the sequence of events at Walsh House.

After supper, the children went upstairs, their laughter trailing behind them like the final notes of a fading melody.

Chrissie with her debut dreams, Petunia with her dolls, and whispered goodnights, Lauren with her book, and Holly and Ivy with their mischief plans. Fox had been awfully quiet during supper. Once Julia's name was cleared, I would need to have a discussion with him.

Only Cosmos and I retired to the drawing room, the fire casting long shadows across the carpet. He nursed a glass of port, his gaze keen behind his spectacles.

"How is Julia, truly? And please don't fob me off with some nonsense."

"She's resting," I replied, keeping my tone even. "She's been through quite a shock."

"And Steele? What's his role in all this?"

"He's helping with the investigation."

He studied me a moment longer but chose not to press. With a quiet grunt, he rose from his chair. "I won't pry tonight. If you need me, you know where to find me."

With that, he withdrew to his study, leaving me alone with the low crackle of the fire and the relentless ticking of the mantel clock.

I waited. And waited. And waited some more. Ten o'clock came, and still no word. At last, with a sigh of resignation, I made my way to my chambers.

Tilly helped me out of my gown, her hands quick and practiced. I had just slipped into my nightgown when a firm knock sounded at the door. Tilly cracked the door open to the footman waiting outside.

"The Duke of Steele is downstairs, milady."

My breath caught. "Tell His Grace I'll be down directly."

With no time for corset and formality, I asked Tilly to help me into a simple gown. As soon as the buttons were fastened, I was hurrying down the stairs, my slippers silent on the carpet, the chill of anticipation rising in my throat.

Steele was waiting in the morning room.

He stood near the hearth, tall and broad-shouldered, dressed in the same unrelenting black that seemed to drink in the dim light around him. His coat was still buttoned against the chill, his gloved hands clasped loosely behind his back, the flicker of the fire casting shadows along the hard planes of his face. He looked like something carved from midnight—elegant, forbidding, and utterly arresting.

The scent of the night clung to him—woodsmoke, damp air, and something indefinably his. It caught me off guard, slipped past my carefully constructed walls, and settled low in my throat.

I had seen him before, countless times. Heard his voice, watched the precision of his movements, studied the mind behind the man. But now, standing here in my home, so near and so completely composed, I saw something else.

He was beautiful.

Not in the way of poets or portraits, but in the way storms are—dark, charged, undeniable.

My breath hitched before I could steady it. And for one unguarded second, I let myself feel the weight of his presence as more than an ally, more than an adversary.

As a man.

CHAPTER
THIRTY-ONE

THE WEIGHT OF THE TRUTH

I stood just inside the doorway, painfully aware of my state—no corset, only a simple gown hastily buttoned, my copper hair pulled into a single braid that hung over one shoulder. I hadn't even taken time to don a shawl. My breathing, no matter how I willed it to slow, remained shallow and uneven.

His gaze found mine—then dropped, just for a moment, to the rise and fall of my chest.

A flicker passed through his expression. Not surprise, exactly. Something sharper. His eyes darkened, and one brow lifted in subtle, unmistakable acknowledgment. My skin prickled beneath the fabric.

Then, as if summoned by some vestige of his better nature, he looked away.

"My apologies," he said, his voice low and rough-edged, "for calling at such a late hour—and for rushing you into a state of ... informal attire."

It was the faintest smile that touched his lips, not quite

smug, not quite sincere. But it made my pulse quicken all the same.

I drew myself up—or tried to, as best one can without a corset—and offered a faint, steady smile. "You came at my invitation, Your Grace. I have no cause to object."

As the chill of the night clung to my skin—I really should have brought a shawl—I stepped inside and let the door click softly shut behind me. Moving past him, I settled into the chair nearest the fire, where the flames crackled in the hearth.

"Tell me about your visit to Walsh House." Of course, he remained standing, one hand resting on the back of the opposite chair. Heaven forbid he should sit down.

Still, I was supremely grateful for the turn to a safer topic—anything to pull us away from the tension simmering between us.

"I wondered if I would be admitted," I said. "But I needn't have worried. Mr. Anstruther, the butler, let me in. Lucretia—Charles's wife—was in her rooms, prostrate with grief."

Steele gave a slow nod. "I've met Anstruther. Old guard. Loyal."

"It was from him I learned the most. The tea that poisoned Charles arrived the day before, around noon. A packet Julia had sent. A housemaid found it later that evening in the morning room. There was a note attached, stating it was to be used for Charles's tea and his alone."

"An odd thing, that," Steele murmured.

"I thought so as well."

"Did the note arrive with the packet?"

"I didn't ask Anstruther." I hesitated. "But Julia wouldn't write something so specific."

"Unless," he said mildly, "she wanted to ensure no one else died from the hemlock."

"She didn't lace it with hemlock!" I shot back, heart quickening.

He lifted a brow. "I'm arguing the other side, Lady Rosalynd."

I exhaled, tense. "The packet was delivered by one of our footmen. He was dressed in Rosehaven House livery."

Steele frowned. "Then there's no chance it was intercepted before arriving at Walsh House."

"None."

A pause.

"So," he said at last, "the poison must have been added after the tea arrived."

"I believe so," I replied. "But the real question is—who would have done it?"

"Who in the house held a grudge against Charles?" Steele asked, his tone low and probing.

"No one. He'd only just arrived. There wasn't time for anyone to turn against him."

"Would someone be so loyal to Julia they would have acted on her behalf?" he pressed.

I shook my head. "I don't see how his death would benefit Julia."

"I can." He remained standing by the fire, his shadow cast long across the hearth rug. The room was dim but for the flickering glow of coals and the sharp glint in his eyes—watchful, calculating, as if fitting puzzle pieces together in real time. "How familiar are you with primogeniture law?"

"Enough to know the basics. The oldest son inherits everything."

He turned to face me fully then, his expression carved from granite. "The title passed to Charles the moment his father breathed his last. As the legitimate firstborn son, he inherited everything."

A chill wrapped around my spine, colder than the night air seeping beneath the windowpanes. "Leaving Julia with nothing," I murmured.

"Unless her late husband left her something in his will," Steele said.

"Which he didn't," I replied. "The only thing she's entitled to is the dower house. But with no annual sum to live on, the inheritance is worthless."

"She was left at Charles's mercy," Steele said grimly.

"But what happens now that Charles is dead?" I asked.

He began to pace again, slowly and deliberately. "If Julia's child is a girl," Steele said, "the title moves to the next male heir—likely a cousin."

"Edwin Heller," I supplied.

"Yes," he confirmed. "But if the child is a boy, and Charles left no issue, then—"

"Her son becomes Lord Walsh," I finished.

He nodded once.

"And all of it would revert to Julia's son?" I asked. "The estate, the house, the fortune?"

"The title, certainly," Steele said. "The entailed properties as well. As for personal wealth—only what remains, and only if it hasn't already been claimed or hidden. But the moment she gives birth to a son, she ceases to be a powerless widow. She becomes the mother of a peer."

The fire hissed softly in the grate, but I no longer felt its warmth. Steele's words echoed in my mind, stark and undeniable. *The mother of a peer*. Not merely a shift in status —an upheaval. A threat. And that would make her a target.

I drew in a slow breath, my fingers curling tightly

around the armrest of my chair. "So that's why she's in danger."

Steele's gaze flicked to mine. He didn't speak—he didn't need to.

"She's gone from an inconvenient widow to the sole guardian of the heir presumptive," I said slowly, as the pieces clicked into place. "If her child is a boy, she holds the key to everything. And if something were to happen to her before the birth ... "

He gave a single, grave nod. "Then the path clears. The title passes to Heller. And he—unlike a newborn—can sign documents. Control land. Shift assets."

I swallowed hard, a fresh wave of unease washing over me. "They wouldn't have to harm the child if Julia didn't live long enough to deliver him."

"If the child is never born," Steele added quietly, "there's nothing to contest."

A silence settled between us, heavy as a funeral shroud.

"All this time," I said, my voice barely more than a whisper, "I thought it was vengeance for funds being stolen. But it wasn't personal, was it?"

"No," Steele replied. "It was business." The word made my skin crawl.

"And business," I murmured, "kills without blinking." I looked up at him. "Edwin Heller murdered Charles."

"And his father before him," Steele said grimly.

I sat back, the air thinning around me as the truth settled in. "Four deaths. There had to be four—Charles's father, then Charles himself ... " I hesitated, the next words catching in my throat. "And then Julia and her unborn child."

The silence that followed was deafening.

"He needed them all gone," I said at last, my voice

unsteady. "Because if even one of them lived, everything would come crashing down around him."

The enormity of it settled over me like a weight. I took a step toward Steele—not out of anger or bravado, but something far more fragile. I needed something solid to hold on to, someone who wouldn't flinch in the face of what I now knew.

The air seemed to thrum, heavy with the weight of all that had passed—and all that might still come. Steele didn't move, but his gaze fixed on mine with unsettling intensity, like a blade held steady in a trembling hand.

Drawn by something I didn't fully understand, I closed the distance between us.

"Rosalynd." He reached for me—not roughly, not in possession, but as if compelled. His fingers curled gently around my throat, a caress more electric than threatening. His thumb brushed across my lower lip, feather-light and devastating. I was suddenly aware of my breathing again—too shallow, too fast—as if my body had remembered its own yearning before my mind had caught up.

Heaven only knew what might have happened next. But a coal dropped in the grate, hissing and crackling as it struck the iron fender, tossing a spray of sparks toward the rug.

We both startled. Just enough to break the spell.

Breath catching, I stepped back as heat rose to my cheeks. The space between us suddenly felt charged in a different way—too close, too exposed. Without a word, I walked away, pretending to busy myself with smoothing my skirts, though my hands trembled slightly. I needed a moment—just one—to collect myself, to remember why we were here. What was at stake.

I drew in a steadying breath and fixed my gaze on the

wallpaper. Still, I couldn't bring myself to turn around. I was afraid of what I'd feel if I looked at him—what I might see reflected in his eyes. The nearness, the heat, the brush of his thumb across my mouth. It all lived too vividly beneath my skin. Needing the quiet to reorder myself, I clung to the silence. But silence, especially with Steele, never stayed quiet for long.

"I should have asked sooner," I said, my voice low. "Did you find Lord Nicholas?"

A pause. Then the shift of fabric as he straightened behind me.

"No," Steele said simply. "I didn't."

I turned back to face him, frowning. "You didn't?"

"I spent the better part of the evening combing through his usual haunts—his club, the gaming rooms in Kensington, even that disreputable little theatre he frequents when the mood strikes. Nothing. Not a word, not a whisper."

His jaw tightened, but only slightly—a flicker of emotion behind the calm. "It's unlike him to disappear without leaving some sort of trail. Even when he's trying to avoid me."

I crossed the room slowly, the sense of dread I'd been pushing aside all evening creeping back in. "Do you think someone's harmed him?"

"I don't know." He looked up at me then, something colder than frustration in his eyes. "But if they have, they'll regret it."

The words hung in the air between us, sharp and absolute.

"How do we prove Edwin Heller committed these murders?" I asked, my voice quieter now, more measured.

"We set a trap."

I crossed my arms, the chill of the room settling through the thin fabric of my gown. "What kind?"

His gaze flicked to the fire, then back to me. "Killers and thieves will do anything for money. That's always been true. You dangle enough of it in front of them, and they reveal who they are."

I studied his face, searching for the thread of a plan.

"You already have something in mind, don't you?"

His mouth curved—just barely. "The bait's already set."

I blinked. "Already?"

"I put the word out earlier tonight. A whisper in the right ear. A suggestion of something valuable. A reward for information."

"You believe someone will come forward?"

"Someone always does. The murderer would have said something to someone. Or someone noticed a newfound wealth.

"How long before you know?"

"I expect to hear something by tomorrow."

He looked at me then—truly looked at me. There was something in his expression I couldn't quite name. Not triumph. Not satisfaction. Something quieter. Protective. Then, without another word, he turned and strode toward the door. He paused, hand on the handle. Glanced back.

I exhaled, tension unspooling in my shoulders. "You'll keep me informed?"

"Of course."

And then he disappeared into the night, leaving only the scent of cold air, woodsmoke, and the lingering echo of something I didn't dare name.

CHAPTER
THIRTY-TWO

THE INFORMANT

The trap had been laid. The bait positioned exactly where it would draw his attention. Now came the part I liked least—waiting.

I paced. Constantly. Not just in moments of tension, but in thought, in habit, in the hollow space between questions and answers. By the time noon came around, I'd nearly worn a track through the carpet in my study at Steele House.

When I wasn't pacing, I was reading. The pages spread out before me weren't aristocratic genealogies or idle reading. They were copies of the latest legislative amendments tied to land inheritance law, marked with notes from three separate clerks. Dry, dense, and crucial. And utterly impossible to concentrate on.

Because all I could think about was Heller.

It wasn't until just past four o'clock that the knock came. Sharp, quick, and not at all in keeping with the usual rhythm of staff or messenger.

Waving away Clifford, I opened the door myself.

The boy on the step couldn't have been more than twelve. Bare-knuckled, sharp-eyed, his cap pulled low over shaggy hair. He didn't speak. Just held out a crumpled piece of paper, pinched between his fingers like it might bite.

I took it and unfolded it.

Spitalfields. Nine o'clock. The Red Hound Tavern.

No signature. None needed. I recognized the hand as one of my informants, the kind who knew better than to write anything more than necessary.

I looked at the boy. "Anything else?"

He shrugged. "Said you'd know."

I gave him a coin. He vanished without another word.

I crossed to my desk and penned a brief note to Rosalynd.

Movement confirmed. Meeting at nine. Will update afterwards. Don't expect me til late.

I signed it with my initials and rang for a trusted footman to deliver it.

Then I turned to the matter of dressing. It had to be something that wouldn't draw a second glance—plain, rough, forgettable. The sort of thing a common man might wear without notice. I rang for my manservant and explained what I needed. He didn't bat an eye. This wasn't the first time I'd gone into the dark under a different face.

The man I needed to be tonight wore threadbare trousers, a coat worn soft with age, and a cap that would not attract undue attention. Nothing that clung to my title. Nothing that would catch the gleam of a streetlamp.

When the time came, my valet rubbed a smear of ash through the white streak above my temple, dulling the mark that too many might recognize or remember. I pulled the cap down low. No one could call me elegant. But it was effective. At the Red Hound, no one looked twice at a man who stayed in the shadows.

At the appointed hour, I took an unmarked hackney and disembarked three streets shy of the tavern. Close enough to watch. Far enough to avoid being seen.

Spitalfields was still, wrapped in the stale fog of supper hour and suspicion. The Red Hound crouched on the corner like something half-forgotten and half-feral.

I stepped inside. It was dim, low-ceilinged, thick with smoke and old beer. The fire burned low. No one looked up.

Good.

I scanned the room—slowly, deliberately. Then I saw him. A man hunched at a table near the back. Ginger hair, dirty around the edges. He sat hunched in the back corner, nursing a pint with both hands, head low, the thatch of red hair catching what little light the hearth gave off.

Benny—my informant—was waiting for me.

I approached slowly, weaving past a pair of drunken labourers and a barmaid who looked like she'd bite before she'd smile.

I stopped just short of the table.

His fingers tightened around a mug of something that smelled like vinegar and regret. I'd recognized him, but it was the nervous twitch in his eyes that gave him away. He was afraid. And he had reason to be.

I slid into the seat across from him. He sniffed as I settled in.

"Gur, Gov'nr," he muttered, nose wrinkling. "Did you pour the whole bleedin' bottle o' perfume on yerself? Smells like a Mayfair brothel in here now."

I let that pass. "Tell me what you saw or heard."

Benny leaned in, glancing over his shoulder before

speaking. "Saw. A toff. He'd been comin' here for weeks. Always quiet. Always polite. Just ... askin' questions."

"What sort of questions?"

"The sort that don't start with murder but end there," he said, voice low. "He'd buy a man a drink, ask what he'd do for coin. Rough work, he'd call it. Nothin' too specific. Not at first."

"And you?"

"I turned him down," Benny said flatly. "Didn't like his eyes. Too clean on the outside, too dead underneath."

"Who was it?"

"Heller."

For a heartbeat, the air left my lungs. My fingers curled into a fist beneath the table, the edge of the wood biting into my palm.

"You're sure it was him?"

"Oh, I'm sure. You don't forget a face like that. Fancy gloves. Talks like a gentleman but never once took off his coat. Like he didn't plan to stay long."

I was quiet a moment. "Did he find someone?"

"Aye. Bloke named O'Donnell. Big, mean, thick as dock mud. Scar down the right side of his face. Always looking for coin. He came in the week before Walsh was found dead. Heller sat with him longer than he did with anyone. Bought him a bottle and a room upstairs. Next day, both of 'em gone."

"Any proof?"

Benny hesitated, then grinned without humor. "I followed 'im."

My brow lifted. "You followed Edwin Heller?"

"I was curious." He shrugged, eyes darting. "Didn't mean to get involved, just ... somethin' felt off. He left out the back and didn't look twice. I tailed him clean to Duke

Street. Nice townhouse, green door, gas lamp out front. Quiet. Real quiet."

That sealed it.

Heller had arranged for Lord Walsh's murder—with coin, not his hands—and now we had a witness.

"You said nothing to anyone?"

"Not unless I wanted to get my throat cut," Benny muttered. "This? What I just told you? It stays between us, Gov'nr. I like breathin'."

I dropped several coins on the table. "Keep liking it."

He slipped out the door without another word.

I waited a minute, then stood. The game was no longer theoretical. And Heller had just run out of places to hide.

I stepped out into the alley behind the Red Hound, keeping to the shadows. Fog clung low to the ground, thick and oily from chimney soot. The coin Benny had taken hadn't even settled in his pocket before I felt the shift—the wrong kind of silence.

Then came the sound.

Not footsteps. *Breath*—fast, too close.

I turned—

Too late.

The blow came from behind, sharp and fast. My shoulder slammed against the brick wall, pain jolting through my arm. I twisted, ducked another swing, and caught a glimpse of him in the gaslight.

O'Donnell. Exactly as Benny described: tall, broad, thick-necked, and built like a butcher.

"Should've minded your business," he growled, raising what looked like a length of lead pipe.

"I'm terribly bad at that," I muttered, drawing the pistol hidden beneath my coat.

He lunged.

The gun fired.

O'Donnell let out a roar of pain and crumpled, clutching his thigh where the bullet had torn through flesh. Just a graze—enough to drop him, not kill him.

Before I could say a word, a whistle shrieked from the end of the alley. A pair of boots pounded closer. A constable rounded the corner, truncheon drawn, eyes wide.

"What's this then?" he barked.

I stepped forward, breath even, pistol lowered but still in hand. "The man you see before you," I said coolly, "is named O'Donnell. He was trying to kill me. He already murdered Lord Walsh. I suggest you place him under arrest—now."

The constable blinked. "And you are?"

I pulled off the cap and stepped into the light. "The Duke of Steele."

That did it.

The constable barked for his partner, who rushed forward. Together they hauled O'Donnell to his feet—bloody, cursing, but alive.

Scotland Yard – Two Hours Later

The room was cramped, the walls scuffed, the gaslight flickering overhead. A constable stood near the door. I stood behind Dodson, arms folded.

O'Donnell slouched in the chair, shirt torn, thigh bandaged, face slack with pain and fatigue.

But his mouth still worked.

"Fine," he growled. "I did it."

Dodson straightened. "You murdered Lord Percival Walsh?"

O'Donnell didn't even blink. "Aye. That's what I was

paid to do. The bloke who hired me gave me all the details. Visited his mistress on Princelet Street Tuesdays and Thursdays."

"Who hired you?"

He hesitated, then sneered. "Edwin bloody Heller. Said it was family business. Said he'd make it worth my while."

I stepped forward, voice quiet and razor-sharp. "And was it?"

O'Donnell looked up at me. "No."

"Why are you confessing?"

"Got the clap, Guv'nr. Ain't got long to live."

The silence that followed was heavy.

The inspector nodded to his detective. "Get it down in writing. Full statement."

O'Donnell spat blood onto the floor. "Glad to." His smile revealed two rows of blackened teeth. "If I'm going to meet my maker. So will he."

CHAPTER
THIRTY-THREE

NO MORE SHADOWS

By the time I left Scotland Yard, the gas lamps were still burning, but the streets were beginning to stir. I hadn't shaved. I couldn't remember if I'd eaten. And I was fairly certain I smelled like a dog's breath after a long night in a butcher's alley.

I went straight to Rosehaven House.

Honeycutt answered the door, as he always did—precise, proper, and impossibly affronted by the sight of me.

He didn't say a word, but his nose wrinkled with impressive eloquence. A single twitch that conveyed a thousand shades of disdain. Still, he stepped aside and gestured me in with all the dignity of a man escorting a chimney sweep into a drawing room.

"Lady Rosalynd is in the morning room," he said. "Waiting for news."

I nodded. "Thank you."

He didn't thank me back.

I made my way down the corridor, the house quiet, the hush of early morning settling in like mist. I pushed open the door and stepped inside.

The fire had burned low, and light from the tall windows had just begun to creep across the floor.

And there she was.

Asleep.

Rosalynd sat curled in one of the armchairs, dressed in another of those plain gowns she favored when no one but family—or me—was likely to see her. A book lay open on her lap, her head tilted to one side, copper hair falling loose from its pins.

She looked exhausted. And lovely. And heartbreakingly vulnerable.

I didn't speak.

Not yet.

I just stood there and watched her breathe.

I crossed the room in silence, my boots making no sound on the rug.

She'd fallen asleep with one hand curled loosely beneath her chin, the other still resting atop an open book. A faint crease lined her brow, even in sleep—like her mind refused to rest fully, even when her body surrendered.

I crouched beside the chair, careful not to startle her. Then, with a tenderness I hadn't allowed myself, I reached out and touched her hand—just the back of it, warm and soft beneath my calloused fingers.

"Rosalynd," I said quietly.

She stirred. Her lashes fluttered, and for a heartbeat she blinked in confusion, as if unsure whether she was waking into the same world she'd fallen asleep in. Then her gaze found mine and cleared.

"Steele," she murmured, voice rough with sleep. "You

look ... " Her eyes swept over me. "Good Lord, you look like you've crawled out of a coal scuttle."

I gave a tired smile. "Close. More like a Spitalfields alley and a holding cell at Scotland Yard."

She sat up straighter, alert now. "What happened?"

"I found your murderer," I said. "And he talked."

She blinked away the last remnants of sleep as her gaze swept over me. And then her eyes narrowed.

"You have blood on your collar," she said. "And heaven knows what's on your coat."

I glanced down. There was indeed a smear of dried blood at my collarbone—likely O'Donnell's, not mine—and my coat, still dusted with alley grime, had seen better centuries.

"I was going for inconspicuous," I said.

"You look like you lost a fight with a chimney," she replied dryly. "And only barely survived."

"Not far off," I said. "But it was O'Donnell who came out worse."

She was on her feet, the last of sleep gone from her face. "O'Donnell attacked you?"

"In an alley behind the tavern. Got a bullet in his leg for the trouble. Just a graze, but enough to stop him."

"You weren't hurt?" Her concern was all for me, rather than the fact the murderer had been found.

"No."

She stared at me a moment, her eyes searching mine. Finally, satisfied with what she saw, she asked, "Did he talk?"

"He did more than that. He confessed."

"Did he, really?"

I nodded. "Heller hired him to kill Walsh. He'd been visiting the Red Hound for weeks, feeling out the regulars.

Asking what they'd be willing to do for coin. Quiet, careful—never saying too much. But my informant saw through it. O'Donnell was the one who took the bait."

"Where is O'Donnell now?"

"In custody. A constable saw the scuffle. We took him to the Yard. He gave a full statement."

Her voice was quiet, razor-sharp. "Heller paid him to kill Walsh."

"He called it a family solution. Said the title, the estate—everything—was slipping away. So he decided to remove the obstacles. One by one."

She exhaled slowly, the weight of it all settling around her. "He would've killed both Julia and her babe."

"But now, he won't get the chance."

"Thank God."

"Yes."

"And you."

CHAPTER
THIRTY-FOUR

REVELATIONS AND RESOLUTIONS

In the days that followed, events unfolded swiftly. Edwin Heller was located, arrested, and formally charged with the murders of both Julia's husband and Charles Walsh. When Dodson had searched Heller's house, he'd discovered a foxglove plant he'd been cultivating. So it wasn't difficult to deduce what had occurred.

Once Charles moved into Walsh House, Heller made a point of visiting his cousin. That's why he was there when Julia's tea packet was delivered. At that point, all he had to do was tuck a few foxglove leaves into the packet before leaving it in the morning room with the note he'd written. Of course, he didn't confess he'd done such a thing. But the testimony of both Steele's informant and O'Donnell damned him. The trial was scheduled in the next week. Given the preponderance of the evidence, he would soon meet justice at the end of a rope.

The entire scheme made perfect sense. First he eliminated Lord Walsh, then Charles. Julia would not have survived long afterward. Heller likely intended her death to appear accidental—a fall down the stairs, perhaps—ensuring both she and her unborn child perished.

Lucretia, who was not increasing, would more than likely have been spared. For the time being, she planned to remain at Walsh House, at least until Julia gave birth. But it Julia's babe was a boy, he would inherit the title and the estate. At that point, Lucretia would have to pack her things and move out. She wouldn't be destitute by any means. Unlike his father, Charles had left her provided for. Given his precarious state of health, he'd arranged a quite comfortable fortune she could live on for many years.

But the greatest surprise of all came from Walsh himself. He had not squandered the investors' money as we all feared. Rather, he'd invested the funds in an American railway venture he'd heard about during a game of cards. The account he'd opened specifically for this venture was at Barings Bank, which had underwritten bonds in the expanding Chicago & North Western Railway. The yields were generous as the American frontier offered the kind of opportunity the English countryside no longer could.

Why he'd chosen to disguise the endeavor as an investment in a silver mine, no one knew. All we could do was guess. Maybe a silver mine sounded like it could provide greater profit, maybe he meant to keep the money for himself. We would never know the reason behind his lies.

What we did know was that the venture was extremely successful. Once the facts became known, the investors were given the opportunity to keep their investments or cash out with interest. Amazingly, most chose to remain in the venture, after confirming that it was indeed a profitable investment.

Though Walsh had made no provision for Julia in his

will, the possibility she carried the heir to the Walsh fortune changed everything. She was granted a generous allowance, enough to establish herself in her dower house and live in comfort. But she chose to remain with us at Rosehaven House until her child was born. It was here she felt safe and dearly loved.

As for Mr. Bellamy, there was no recourse for recovering his gambling losses. Lord Walsh had won the money over a game of cards. Whether it was fair and square or Walsh had cheated him did not come into it.

Though his prospects had seemed grim, fortune had seen fit to smile upon him as he'd managed to win the affection of a wealthy heiress. Her father, wisely cautious, insisted on securing her dowry with legal protections Bellamy could not breach. In the end, he would live in comfort, even if his path to it had been riddled with missteps. One could only hope he'd learned from his mistakes.

Life at Rosehaven House soon returned to its familiar rhythm. The scent of fresh bread wafted from the kitchens each morning, petitions for charitable support once more filled my study desk, and the younger girls as well as Fox continued their lessons with their usual mix of mischief and complaint. On the surface, everything was as it had always been.

And yet ... it wasn't.

Where once I had found comfort in these routines, now they felt oddly hollow. I moved through each day with the same diligence, the same sense of duty. But there was a quiet ache I could not name. A space within me that had not existed before, or perhaps one I had never noticed until it was stirred awake.

The truth was, I missed Steele.

Not just his brooding silences and sudden flashes of sardonic wit, but the way he had made the world seem sharper, more alive. He had stirred something within me I could not easily dismiss. And now, with the case resolved, with justice served and Julia safe beneath my roof, he was gone.

I told myself it was inevitable.

But the question that haunted me now was far more unsettling. Could I truly go on as before, knowing what it felt like to live in the light of his presence?

I had no answer. Only the silence of the morning room and the soft ticking of the mantel clock to keep me company.

Until the door burst open.

"Rosie!" Chrissie cried, her cheeks flushed with excitement. "She's here—the modiste! And you *must* come at once. The gown for the Duchess of Comingford's ball has arrived, and it's even lovelier than we imagined!"

She flew across the room like a spring breeze, her energy scattering my melancholy like so many leaves. "Shall I fetch Julia?" she asked, barely pausing for breath. "She might enjoy a bit of distraction. And I daresay she could use a glimpse of something beautiful."

I rose, smoothing my skirts with a practiced hand. "Yes," I said, grateful for something—anything—that would keep the shadows at bay. "Ask if she feels up to it."

Chrissie beamed. "Oh, she will. She needs this as much as you do."

And with that, she was gone again, her footsteps pattering down the corridor, leaving the door swinging behind her like a punctuation mark on a sentence I hadn't realized was ending.

Life carried on, ready or not.

Soon, Rosehaven was abuzz with preparations for the ball. Gowns were pressed, gloves sorted, and jewels laid out with care. It was to be the event of the season, a night of elegance and spectacle.

And I, like it or not, would be at the very center of it.

Not because I craved attention—far from it. But in the wake of the scandal surrounding Lord Walsh's murder, and my all-too-visible role in the investigation alongside the Duke of Steele, I could hardly expect to pass unnoticed. Society would be watching, their whispers sharp as hatpins. I would be observed, dissected, judged.

I would have gladly missed the entire affair.

But there was no help for it. Chrissie had been looking forward to the ball for weeks, and she deserved her moment in the sun—unshadowed by murder, scandal, or grief.

For her sake, I would go. And I would smile.

No matter what the night might bring.

CHAPTER
THIRTY-FIVE

THE LAST WALTZ

The marble beneath our feet gleamed like still water, reflecting the brilliance of the ballroom chandeliers below. The grand staircase of Comingford House stretched out before us, less an entrance than a stage upon which, like it or not, we were about to perform.

"Her Grace, the Dowager Countess of Rosehaven," the majordomo announced, his voice ringing down the gilded hall, "Lady Rosalynd Rosehaven, and Lady Chrysanthemum Rosehaven."

At once, the ballroom fell silent.

Not the elegant hush of music fading or dancers pausing politely, but a stunned, breathless quiet, as if the entire assembly had collectively forgotten how to blink. Heads turned. Fans drooped. A few glasses were set down with audible clinks. The air thrummed with the weight of gossip barely restrained.

At my side, Grandmother inhaled, drawing herself to

full height, chin tilted with majestic disdain. "Well," she said in a voice dry as vintage sherry, "either they think we've come to confess, or to start another scandal."

Chrissie let out a tiny squeak beside me. I bit the inside of my cheek to keep from smiling.

And then, with poise borrowed from generations of scandal-surviving women before us, we began our descent.

Waiting at the bottom, precisely centered beneath the great arch of the ballroom entrance, stood Her Grace, the Duchess of Comingford.

Resplendent in midnight blue silk and diamond drops that glinted like frost, she stood as still as a statue—though her eyes were anything but frozen. They scanned each of us as we approached, taking in Grandmother's steel spine, Chrissie's fragile composure, and whatever expression I'd managed to fix in place.

As we reached the final step, she moved forward.

"Countess," the Duchess said with a nod. "Lady Rosalynd. Lady Chrysanthemum."

"Your Grace," Grandmother replied, offering her hand with the faintest dip of her chin. "A splendid turnout. Nothing draws a crowd like murder, I always say."

The Duchess's lips twitched. "Quite. Though I admit, I'm pleased to see you here." She nodded toward me. "Lady Rosalynd."

I met her gaze squarely as I curtsied. "You doubted we would come?"

"I hoped you would," she said. "There's nothing quite so effective at killing rumor as being seen, is there?"

"No," I said, my voice even. "But sometimes being seen only makes the whispers louder."

Her smile deepened, though whether it was amusement or admiration, I couldn't say. "Then I trust you'll give them something worth whispering about." She paused, eyes glinting just a touch. "And do let me know when the Society for the Advancement of Women next convenes. I find myself increasingly tempted to attend."

Beside me, Grandmother made a faint sound—possibly a scoff, possibly a chuckle.

"I'll see that your name is added to the list," I said, unable to keep the corner of my mouth from lifting.

The Duchess inclined her head. "Please do." Stepping aside with practiced grace, she motioned us into a shimmering sea of lace and silk and the weight of a hundred curious stares.

We'd barely taken a few steps when a tidal wave of suitors in crisply tailored jackets descended upon Chrissie—all of them clamoring to be the first on her card. Their smiles were eager as their voices overlapped in a flurry of polite desperation.

"Lady Chrysanthemum, might I claim the first waltz?"

"Surely you've saved the quadrille for me, milady—"

"I've a cousin who will be green with envy if I secure a set tonight—"

Chrissie laughed, a sound so light and bright it made me smile. With poise far beyond her years, she began jotting names onto her card, smiling graciously at each new request, her dance card filling faster than champagne glasses.

I watched from just beyond the swirling edge of satin and silk. Her cheeks were flushed with delight, her eyes shining. For the first time in weeks, she could truly enjoy herself without the weight of scandal.

Grandmother leaned in, her voice dry as ever. "If any of them propose before supper, I do hope you've remembered to pack the Rosehaven emeralds."

I gave her a sidelong glance. "Chrissie is not so silly as to accept a marriage proposal without consulting me first."

One arched brow signaled Grandmother's skepticism.

"And naturally," I added, "we'd speak to Cosmos. As the head of the family, he would never allow one of his sisters to marry anyone less than worthy."

Grandmother gave a faint, noncommittal hum.

"He'd look into everything," I went on. "The family and the bank accounts, of course. But more than that, the gentleman's character and integrity. And most of all, whether he could be trusted to care for her the way she deserves."

Grandmother gave the barest nod, just enough to acknowledge the truth of it. "Well," she murmured, "he *is* your father's son."

We both looked again toward Chrissie, radiant at the edge of the dance floor, fielding admirers with gentle charm and unshakable poise. For once, she didn't seem the least bit fragile.

From the corner of her eye, Grandmother caught sight of a familiar cluster of bejeweled matrons arranged like artillery along a row of gilt-backed chairs.

"Ah," she murmured, "the Dowager Battalion is fully deployed this evening. Lady Pellham at the helm, naturally. I suppose I ought to report in before one of them declares me absent without leave."

I suppressed a smile. "Do try to behave."

Grandmother sniffed. "Among that lot? I shall consider it an act of diplomacy if I don't skewer someone with my cane."

Then, with all the dignity of a retiring general and none of the subtlety, she leaned into her ivory-handled cane and swept off into the ballroom—majestic, unsinkable, and entirely in command of her troops.

With Chrissie twirling deeper into a sea of satin and suitors, and Grandmother gone to join the Dowager Battalion, I found myself momentarily adrift.

I moved forward into the ballroom at a measured pace, not seeking anyone in particular, only weaving through the swell of music and murmurs, nodding here and there in acknowledgment of familiar faces. An aging viscountess lifted her lorgnette and offered a stiff smile. A junior baron gave a slight bow, clearly more curious than courteous. I met each glance with composed detachment, my expression polite.

It wasn't that I was trying to avoid being seen. I knew better than to disappear in a room like this. But I wasn't quite ready to be found, either. I had nearly reached the far side of the ballroom when a gloved hand caught my elbow.

"Well," came a familiar voice—dry as champagne and twice as effervescent—"that was quite an entrance. I couldn't have done better myself."

I turned to find Claire at my side, a twinkle in her eye and an expression that suggested she'd just witnessed the scandalous first act of a particularly delicious play.

"I didn't intend to make an entrance."

"But you did nonetheless." She gestured toward the onlookers with her fan. "You have a way of captivating them, Rosalynd. And the most maddening part? You don't even realize it."

Eager to turn the conversation in another direction, I suggested, "Can we please change the subject?"

"Of course." Her gaze swept the ballroom like a hawk scanning the ground for movement. "Lady Litchfield is wearing last season's Worth gown. I'd stake my reputation on it. And Lord Beaufort has just asked Miss Dering to dance again, which means either he's in love or hoping to marry her and her fabulous dowry."

She took a sip of champagne, her eyes twinkling with mischief. "Lady Farnsworth arrived late—very flushed—with her 'cousin' in tow. Not the same one as last week, mind you."

I couldn't help it. I laughed. "How do you know all this?"

Claire gave a mock sigh. "Because I don't spend my time pretending I don't care what people say. I *listen*. Radical, I know." Her gaze flicked casually toward the dance floor. "Oh, and your duke is here. Has been for at least twenty minutes."

My breath hitched. "If you mean Steele, he's not *my* duke."

"Mmm." She swirled the liquid in her glass. "He hasn't danced once, which makes him either incredibly intimidating or exceedingly choosy. Possibly both."

I didn't look. Not yet. The mere mention of him had stirred something tight and fluttering beneath my ribs, and I refused to let Claire see it.

Naturally, she saw it anyway. "Oh, darling," she said, smirking, "do stop pretending you haven't been scanning every corner of this ballroom since you descended those stairs. You could've lit a fire with the tension between you two at Lady Walsh's ball. And that was before you began skulking about together, investigating Walsh's murder."

She leaned in, voice deliciously conspiratorial. "I can only imagine what you got up to. Visiting each other's homes. Dropping into that little house in Chelsea—the very one his father used for liaisons with his mistress."

I blinked. "What?"

"You didn't know?" Her brows rose in mock innocence. "The old duke bought it for his paramour. Quite the scandal, back in the day. *Your* Steele never used it. Until you. For your tryst."

"It was not a *tryst*," I snapped just a shade too loudly, which, of course, made a few heads turn.

I gave her a withering look. "Are you quite finished?"

"Almost." She leaned in again, her tone turning light, almost offhand. "Tell me. Where is Cosmos this evening?"

"Claire," I said warningly, "you promised."

"I did, didn't I?" she mused. "Well, you'll be pleased to know I've taken up a new interest."

"Other than gossip, you mean?"

"Yes. Plants. Oh, and flowers too. I've joined the Royal Society for Botanical Inquiry."

I turned my head slowly toward her. "That's the association Cosmos belongs to."

"Is it really?" she asked, eyes alight with unholy amusement.

Before I could form a suitably scathing response to Claire's botanical ambitions, a familiar voice—low, velvet-edged, unmistakably his—cut through the din of the ballroom like a blade sliding through silk.

"Lady Rosalynd."

It was absurd, really, how quickly the world seemed to hush. Not in volume, perhaps, but in clarity. As though every note of the orchestra, every rustle of silk, every murmured aside faded into nothing beneath the weight of his voice.

Unable to prevent myself, I turned toward him.

He stood, tall and composed in formal black, a white waistcoat lending sharp contrast to his dark presence. The Duke of Steele. The man who had haunted my dreams, disturbed my composure, and—at this very moment—looked at me as though nothing and no one else in the room existed.

He bowed, perfectly correct as the occasion called for it. "Would you do me the honor of this next dance?"

Claire didn't bother to hide her grin.

As he extended his hand, I hesitated for only a breath. And then I placed mine in his without a word, acutely aware of the warmth of his palm against my glove and the subtle strength behind his restraint. We moved together onto the floor just as the orchestra swelled into the first notes of a waltz.

He guided me into motion with practiced ease—no hesitation, no misstep, as though we'd been dancing together our entire lives. The scent of vetiver, cut with a whisper of bergamot, clung faintly to him, threaded with something darker—leather, perhaps—and the coolness of night air.

"You're quiet," he said, after a moment.

"I'm thinking," I replied, eyes fixed somewhere in the distance. "It's what I do when I'm not being accused of trysts or plotting scandals ."

He let out a quiet breath of something that might have been amusement. Then, after a beat, he said, "You're looking lovely tonight."

My gaze engaged with his. "Is that flattery or reconnaissance?"

"Observation."

He turned us in a slow, deliberate sweep across the polished floor, and for a moment the world blurred—crystal chandeliers spinning, silk skirts brushing past, candlelight catching on sequins and diamonds. But all I could feel was the press of his hand at my back and the weight of that single word hanging in the space between us.

"Thank you," I said at last, more breath than voice.

He nodded once, his expression unreadable. "It's not a compliment, Rosalynd. It's a fact."

For a time, we moved in silence. The music swelled around us, a graceful veil between the present and all that had come before. I was aware only of the warmth of his hand at my back, the rhythm of his breath, and the way he seemed to steady the world by simply being near.

Then his voice, low and even, cut through the hush. "How is your cousin?"

"She's well," I said, lifting my gaze to meet his. "She's still at Rosehaven House—for now. The doctor insists she stay close to comfort, not chaos. Only trusted friends are allowed to visit her. She's content to wait out the birth in peace."

A beat passed. Then, more softly, he asked, "And after the child is born?"

"If it's a boy, she'll claim all that's due her son—title, estate, the protections that come with both. If it's a girl . . ." I hesitated. "She'll retire to the dower house. Quietly. The funds we uncovered through the investigation will be enough for her to live well."

He studied my face, searching for something. "Will she remarry, you think?"

"She might. In time. But it's far from her mind at the moment."

He was silent again for several beats, guiding me through a long turn. The music spun around us, but everything inside me had gone still. There was no danger now— no hunt, no shadow pressing in.

"She's stronger than most gave her credit for," I said quietly.

"So are you."

There was something in his voice—low, almost reverent—that I wasn't ready to face. Not here. Not now.

I turned away under the pretense of surveying the ballroom, letting my gaze drift across the sea of glittering gowns and tailored coats. In the distance, I spotted Lord Nicholas in conversation with his mother, the Duchess of Steele. Both were watching us with thinly veiled interest.

I inclined my head in their direction. "Lord Nicholas appears to have recovered his spirits."

"He has," Steele replied. "A bit of solitude at the Richmond estate did him good."

"And perhaps a word or two from his elder brother?"

"I may have suggested he was making a cake of himself."

My lips curved despite myself, though I kept any reply to myself. Amusement warred with the strange ache low in my chest—a feeling I had no desire to name.

The music softened, signaling the end of the set. Steele's hand lingered at my back for the briefest moment before he stepped away just enough to meet my gaze.

"There's a conservatory just off the ballroom," he said quietly. "Glass walls, warm air, and a few thriving orchids. It's quiet enough to talk—without giving the gossips anything new to whisper about."

It was a thoughtful offer, beautifully calculated. I ached to say yes. To follow him into that warm, green quiet and let the rest of the world melt away.

But as I glanced across the ballroom, I caught sight of Chrissie—laughing up at her dance partner, cheeks flushed, eyes alight with something close to joy. She looked radiant, untouched by scandal for the first time in weeks.

I couldn't risk drawing attention now.

"I appreciate the offer," I said, keeping my voice steady. "But I can't. This is Chrissie's night. I won't risk turning it into mine."

Steele studied me for a moment, his gaze unreadable. Then, with a nod of quiet understanding, he stepped back.

"Another time, then."

"Perhaps," I said, knowing how badly I wished it could be now.

He disappeared once more into the press of silk and music, leaving behind the echo of his touch and a truth I could no longer deny.

I remained where I was, still and composed amid the swirl of music and motion, but inside, everything trembled.

How I wanted to follow him. Not for secrecy or scandal or some foolish romantic thrill, but for something far quieter—and far more dangerous.

I wanted to sit beside him in the soft warmth of that conservatory. To speak plainly. To rest, if only for a moment, in the company of someone who had seen me at my sharpest, my most determined, and still called me *lovely*.

It wasn't just desire. It was *peace* I longed for. The kind of peace I had spent my entire adult life denying myself in service to duty, reputation, and the ever-watchful eyes of society. I had not allowed myself to dream of tenderness, of partnership—not really. And yet, with him, I'd begun to.

But I couldn't afford the indulgence. Not while Chrissie's name still hung in the balance, not while Petunia still needed my steadiness, not while the Rosehaven legacy rested so heavily on my shoulders.

So I stood still, spine straight, chin lifted, and let the moment pass me by like so many others.

Perhaps, one day, I would be free to reach for what my heart most desired.

But tonight, I was Lady Rosalynd Rosehaven—sister, protector, and scandal's most unwilling shadow. The conservatory would remain empty.

I turned away from the dance floor, weaving through the crowd until I found Claire exactly where I'd left her— standing, still smug, and sipping her champagne with all the elegance of a cat watching a bird try to escape a cage.

She didn't even wait for me to say anything. "He asked you for a moment of privacy, didn't he?"

I slid next to her. "Are you a lip reader now?"

"I didn't have to be," she said, setting her glass down on a passing waiter's tray with a delicate clink. "I read his face. And yours. You turned him down."

I looked away. "I have obligations, Claire."

She didn't say anything at first. Just picked up another champagne flute, tilted it toward the chandelier, and let the bubbles catch the light. Then, softly but without apology: "You're a fool."

I didn't disagree. Not because she was cruel. But because she was right.

Across the ballroom, Chrissie danced in a swirl of pale silk, her face alight—radiant with promise. I watched her twirl and laugh and shine, and I reminded myself—again— why I had chosen duty over desire.

But just before I looked away, I saw him.

Steele stood at the edge of the crowd, half in shadow, his eyes fixed on mine. He didn't smile. He didn't beckon. He simply watched with the quiet sorrow of a man who had been denied what I could not bear to give.

And then, as the orchestra swelled into another waltz, he disappeared into the glittering throng.

EPILOGUE

A MONTH LATER

It was a rare thing—a warm, golden day in mid-spring when London felt more like a promise than a burden.

Taking advantage of the fine weather, the children and I strolled to Grosvenor Square for a few hours of play. They dashed about with shrieks of delight while I lingered on a bench beneath a budding plane tree, a novel resting open on my lap, forgotten.

The square was alive with laughter and conversation, carriages gliding past the railings and nannies gossiping beneath parasols. It was all so familiar. So wonderfully, achingly ordinary.

But, as I looked up, something shifted.

Across the square, near the west gate, stood a figure I knew instantly. Tall, dark, self-contained. The cut of his coat, the set of his shoulders. Steele. And he was not alone.

A young lady in a deep green walking suit stood beside him, speaking with animation. Her curls caught the light as she tilted her head and smiled up at him. I recognized her.

Lady Scarlet. Lord Throckmorton's daughter. A beauty, undeniably. And a noted heiress besides.

Steele inclined his head as she spoke, his expression unreadable from this distance.

I told myself it didn't matter. But my heart clenched all the same.

Not out of jealousy. I had no claim on him, after all. But out of the quiet, bitter realization that something had changed within me. Something I could no longer deny. But whatever had grown between us had ended at the Duchess of Comingford's ball. And I had no one to blame but myself.

I turned back to my book, where I spent several minutes not taking in any words. But then, a cry alerted me to a change.

"Duke!" Petunia's voice rang out across the square, clear and insistent. "We're playing Skittles and I just knocked over *seven!* Would you like to join us?"

I looked up in surprise to find Steele crossing the lawn toward us, the sunlight catching the faintest gleam at his temple. He bowed with mock solemnity at Petunia's invitation.

"Seven, you say?" he replied gravely. "A formidable score. I doubt I can match it."

She beamed. "You may try! I'll even let you go next."

Steele crouched beside the wooden pins, inspecting the setup with the seriousness of a man reviewing battlefield plans. "High stakes," he murmured, his gaze flicking sideways toward me. "Lady Rosalynd."

For one suspended moment, everything else—Lady Scarlet, the spring air, even my aching heart—fell away.

He smiled, faint but unmistakable. "May I?"

I found my voice at last. "Only if you're prepared to be thoroughly trounced by a seven-year-old."

He settled into the game with the children, unbothered by the stares of passing matrons or the indignity of kneeling on the grass beside a crooked wooden frame.

I watched them for a moment, then rose and joined them, knowing full well the gossip this scene might stir. But I no longer cared. At least not entirely.

Did you enjoy *A Murder in Mayfair*? If you did, I invite you to take a look at *A Murder in Trinity Lane*, Book 2 in the Rosalynd & Steele Mysteries.

A forbidden passion. A dangerous secret. A truth some would kill for to keep buried.

London, 1889. Hoping society has begun to forget the scandal that once engulfed her, **Lady Rosalynd Rosehaven** turns her attention to one of her most cherished causes—the Home for Unwed Mothers, a discreet refuge where poor, unmarried women can give birth in safety and dignity. But when one of the young women is found murdered in a shadowed alley off Trinity Lane, the fragile calm of Rosalynd's aristocratic life is abruptly shattered.

Drawn into the case by a desperate plea, Rosalynd reluctantly turns to the one man she swore to keep at arm's length—the enigmatic **Duke of Steele**. Brilliant, brooding, and far too perceptive for her comfort, Steele stirs emotions she has fought hard to suppress. Their uneasy alliance soon leads them deep into a tangled web of hidden pasts, threatened reputations, and powerful figures determined to protect their secrets—no matter the cost.

As pressure builds from both the high society drawing rooms and the shadows of power, Rosalynd must risk everything—her reputation, her safety, and a part of herself she never wished to surrender. In seeking justice, she may lose more than her good name. She may lose her heart.

A Murder in Trinity Lane, Book 2 in the **Rosalynd & Steele Mysteries** by *USA Today* bestselling author Magda Alexander, plunges readers into a world of forbidden passions, deadly secrets, and Victorian suspense. Perfect for fans of historical mystery series featuring independent women sleuths, brooding dukes, and slow-burn romance, this Victorian historical mystery will keep readers riveted until the final page.

CAST OF CHARACTERS

The Rosehaven Family

Lady Rosalynd Hartwell - Our heroine, sister to the Earl of Rosehaven

Cosmos - the Earl of Rosehaven, Rosalynd's older brother

Lords William and Fox - Rosalynd's younger brothers

Ladies Chrysanthemum ("Chrissie"), Laurel, Holly and Ivy (twins), and last but not least, Petunia - Rosalynd's younger sisters

The Rosehaven Household

Tilly Dodd - Lady Rosalynd's maid
Maisie Flanagan – the downstairs maid
Mister Honeycutt - the Rosehaven butler
Mrs. Bateman - the Rosehaven housekeeper

The Steele Family

CAST OF CHARACTERS

Warwick Thornburn - the Duke of Steele
Lord Nicholas - the Duke of Steele's younger brother
The Dowager Duchess of Steele

Duke of Steele Household

Mister Milford - the Steele butler

Other Notable Characters

Lady Julia Walsh - Lady Rosalynd's cousin
Lord Percival Walsh - Lady Walsh's husband
Charles Walsh - Lord Walsh's son by his first wife
Lucretia Walsh- Charles Walsh's wife
Edwin Heller - Charles Walsh's cousin
Inspector Dodson from Scotland Yard

This book is a work of fiction. All names, characters, locations, and incidents are products of the author's imagination, or have been used fictitiously. Any resemblance to actual persons living or dead, locales, or events is entirely coincidental.

Copyright © 2025 by Amalia Villalba

All rights reserved.

The uploading, scanning, and distribution of this book in any form or by any means—including but not limited to electronic, mechanical, photocopying, recording, or otherwise—without the permission of the copyright holder is illegal and punishable by law. Please purchase only authorized editions of this work, and do not participate in or encourage electronic piracy of copyrighted materials. Your support of the author's rights is appreciated.

ISBN-13: (EBook) 978-1-943321-43-8

ISBN-13: (Print) 978-1-943321-49-0

Hearts Afire Publishing

Printed in Dunstable, United Kingdom